Accidental Baby For My Brother's Best Friend

An Age Gap Rockstar Romance

Callie Stevens

Chapter 1

Locke

"*A tour*, Locke, did you hear me?"

Jackson Arden shakes my shoulder as if I were deaf instead of just staring at him blankly.

"Who the hell would give us a tour?" I ask, gratefully taking the tequila shot when the bartender slides it to me.

Jackson's proud grin tells me the answer before he speaks. "My baby sister. She raised the money."

"Gemma?" I try to keep the disbelief out of my voice, but Jackson rolls his eyes.

"Don't act surprised. She's been managing Jack and the Spades since she turned eighteen. She's like a prodigy or something."

I hum in response. It isn't as if I don't know Gemma has done a lot to market our band and get us the best gigs. Hell, she had somehow gotten our social media up to twenty thousand followers while we were still playing in dive bars. Gemma is capable, that's for sure, but she is also a whopping twenty-one years old. They say age is just a number, but come on. This number shows she is even barely allowed

1

to drink, how can she be responsible for our future as a band?

"Don't be a jerk, Kincaid. It's exciting! We're even booked in Vegas!" Jackson chugs from his big bottle of water, never one to drink before shows. I can't relate - big crowds make me nervous. Fame has never been my main goal - I live to make music. I never had big aspirations to be a famous musician - that's more Jackson's style. I'm a drummer, I'd be happy enough just to be playing at dive bars if nothing else. What's really important to me is doing what I love. It's nice to have fans, don't get me wrong, but the possibility of failure when there's thousands of fans rather than hundreds...that scares me.

At my age, hitting it big didn't seem like much of a possibility - at least until Jackson came along with his little sister in tow, about half my size but twice the personality.

A tour means that Gemma's big personality is getting us somewhere, and while I'm still nervous, I have to admit it's also exciting.

As if she knows I'm thinking about her, Gemma swings open the back door of the bar, like she owns the place, with the most serious look on her face, her button nose scrunched up.

"Locke," she greets icily.

I look away when she meets my eyes, signaling the bartender for a beer that I'll take on stage, and Gemma lets out a breath in a huff. It almost makes me want to smile, but I force it back down.

Gemma Arden is cute and all—okay, fine, more than cute—but at a little more than ten years younger than me, I am not about to let myself look too long - especially since she is Jackson's sister and Jackson is family to me. Also, those two come from a superior gene pool when it comes to looks. Deep brown with hints of auburn, Gemma's hair has begun to grow out since the last time I saw her a few months ago. Past her shoulders, it bounces when she walks, and the hints of red often catch my eye underneath the lowlights of the bars we always play in. Not that I look at her that closely, of course. Not much, anyway.

She and Jackson both share wide eyes with long lashes, a pale green that seems striking on stage for Jackson and a little intimidating from Gemma. She never did like me much.

At barely nineteen., and me closing in on the dreaded three oh, she thought she knew best. And maybe she did. I mean, she did get us a tour, right? But she never even tried listening to what my experience could teach her. I get it. They were used to having to fend for themselves since she and Jackson had a rough go of it after their parents died when they were teens.

I can relate, but it was more that I got kicked out at sixteen because my parents weren't nearly as supportive as Jackson's had been. Nevertheless, with Jackson, our similar backgrounds of growing up too quickly made us fast friends...it just isn't the same with Gemma. I'd already been drumming for various bands and in my own garage for years before I tried out for Jack and the Spades, so I have my own ideas about the gigs we should book. Gemma, however, had already taken on the role of manager by the time we met, so we tend to butt heads a lot. I won't even mention how we were in the beginning.

Still, I'd like to think we have a tenuous truce, but Gemma still mostly ignores me *and* my advice.

I see her in my peripheral vision, leaning over the bar and ordering her signature drink: a filthy vodka martini, no vermouth, just olive juice, well shaken.

The first time I'd heard her order it on her twenty-first birthday, I'd made a face.

"Filthy? That's a hell of a drink for an innocent," I *cracked, and she smirked at me.*

"Who's innocent?" she shot back.

I have to admit that her answer had intrigued me, just a little. Hell, maybe Gemma Arden intrigues me a little in general, despite my best interests.

The forbidden fruit and all that, right?

My particular weakness isn't girls who fawn all over me just because I know how to flip a set of drumsticks. I enjoy the chase. And Gemma can most definitely provide that kind of excitement. The fact that she's my best friend's little sister should be a deterrent, and kind of is, but what can I say?

I'm a musician, with all that pertains, after all, and Gemma is sassy and easy on the eyes - just my type, unfortunately. Especially since if Jackson figures out I have less than innocent thoughts about his baby sister, he'll probably break my fingers. Or my arms and legs. Or bury me somewhere off path.

So I keep my mouth shut, and my eyes down, and she runs the show. She's run it well for the two years that she's managed with me in the band, even if we do have our differences.

Jackson bounces off to talk to the bar owner. He is such a social butterfly, a true lead singer. His voice has a particularly rough quality that fits well with the indie rock music we produce. He's a hell of a songwriter too, so it's no wonder that we are doing well. And as exciting as it is, like I said, our success makes me a bit nervous. Because there is more risk that something can go wrong, and there is no way to imagine my life without music.

Music is the only thing that I've ever been *good* at, and even if it wasn't, it's the only thing I do that really feels like *me* and not just some projection of what other people want to see. Like my parents did. Like my ex did...No, not going there. Besides, it doesn't matter anymore, because this is who I really am. And right now, there's a certain pretty distraction leaning over the bar and I couldn't be prouder of myself for not glancing down at the scoop neck of her dress. See? I'm a *gentleman*, not just a drummer.

"How'd you manage to raise enough money for a tour?" I ask, and I don't know if I'm really curious or if I just want to find out what it's like to have a normal conversation with Gemma.

"Wouldn't you like to know?" she teases, but she gives me a genuine smile. And I'm breathless for a second. It makes me wish I'd taken a second shot of tequila instead of a beer to take on stage.

I probably should have kept quiet, but I can't help myself. I raise an eyebrow, and Gemma laughs, loud and open, those green eyes sparkling.

I look down into my beer again as she speaks. This care-free Gemma is having an unexpected effect on me. Not good.

"We've been getting a great turnout at these downtown lounges, so I put away twenty percent of the money."

"That's smart," I reply without thinking, and when I look up at her, she tilts her head, looking baffled.

"A compliment? From Locke Kincaid?"

I scoff. "Don't let it go to your head, little bit."

Gemma's happy expression turns into a scowl, and this time, I can't help but grin. Scowling Gemma I can handle just fine. She's a lot less easygoing than Jackson, with her dogged determination, and it's fun to rile her up.

Callie Stevens

The bartender taps my arm, pointing at the music dials on the wall to ask if we're ready for soundcheck, and I count my lucky stars that I'm saved from thinking of more ways to rile up Gemma Arden. Or to make her smile again.

Because that can only lead to a wreck. Been there, done that, thank you very much.

Chapter 2

Gemma

Watching my brother perform has always been the best part of this job. Well, that, and I can't deny the rest of the Spades are *serious* eye-candy.

I can admit that my brother is attractive. After all, we share the same genes and I'm pretty damn cute myself, or so guys tell me, but the other members...well, they're something else.

Ranking in number one in looks and talent, in my opinion, is the lead guitarist: Axel Jermaine. This rank does not include my brother, for obvious reasons. He is the most talented person in the world and as attractive as he may be, he is still my brother, so, yuck. Anyway, currently, Axel is performing Eric Clapton's infamous guitar solo from "Layla" and my eyes are fixed on him as if under a spell.

"He has such talented fingers," a girl standing near me all but screeches, and a smile spreads across my face. I look over at her and realize that she's one of the Spades' "groupies," one of the girls (along with some guys) who follow the band around from dive bar to dive bar, city to city. Their fans are pretty chill, as they go, but they're predominantly young women, of course, and some of the guys can be easily distracted. Sometimes, I get irritated with having to act as a potential bouncer, but I'm in such a good mood tonight that I don't even feel slightly annoyed.

"I bet," I drawl, laughing a little, and even though I know he can't have possibly heard the exchange over the music and amps, Axel's blue eyes meet mine and he drops a slow wink at me.

Not one to be outdone (or possibly faint as the blonde next to me might have), I wink back, biting the corner of my lip, and Axel grins back widely.

My eyes move from his face to his right forearm as he finishes up the solo. Axel has never revealed what his tattoos mean, and I am more than curious about them, truth be told. Axel and I became close friends almost right away, both being extroverted and a little too blunt at times.

My brother would skin Axel for just that wink if he wasn't distracted crouching down on the front stage, crooning out the lyrics to a redhead in the front row. Besides, I'm busy enough keeping my brother on the straight and narrow as well as managing his band. I'm not actually interested in dating Axel, or anyone for that matter, but it can be fun now and again to flirt.

The bassist gives me a big open smile as I weave my way to the front to adjust one of the spotlights that appears to be shining directly in his face, and I grin back with a little wave. Sam blushes and I'm endeared, as always. Samuel Hansen is the "baby" of the group, and even though he's four years older than me, he does seem younger. Sam is a sweetheart, though, much different than the rest of the group...especially the drummer, Locke Kincaid.

I reach over, pushing the spotlight slightly to get it out

of Sam's eyes, and he nods at me gratefully as they start the opening bars of "Baba O'Riley" by The Who.

The first few songs they perform are covers, of course, because all these dive bars have a certain vibe that they expect Jack and the Spades to form into. That will all change when the tour comes, and I'm so excited about it that I can barely contain myself. My brother and I have been writing songs together since we were kids - or at least, since *I* was a kid, and I've had a hand in penning some of the lyrics of Jack and the Spades' songs. Of course, I never told any of the others that, because Jackson and I do it together, and it's *his* dream, not mine.

I'm not sure if I have any dreams. Not exactly, anyway. I just want to make sure that Jackson is happy and successful and pay him back for all he's done for me after our parents passed so suddenly. If life has taught me anything, it's that nothing ever lasts forever. And I'm happy doing what I'm doing. So, I'll continue doing it and making Jackson's dream come true until I find my own. And I wish mom and dad were here to see it.

No, I don't want to think about my parents right now. My first filthy martini is down the hatch and my second is sloshing around as I sway to the music, moving back to the middle of the crowd so that I'm not in the spotlight.

It's not that I mind being the center of attention, it's just that I want the band to stand on its own, and although they have captured the attention of nearly every woman in the bar, the scouts that we're looking for in terms of record deals, the ones I email every week without fail, are mostly male.

I guess the saying is true: it *is* a man's world.

Jack and the Spades *are* talented, and I don't just say that because my brother is the lead singer. Axel and Sam

9

can play both lead and bass guitar so that they sometimes swap parts, and even though I'm loath to admit it, Locke is a damn good drummer.

I sigh heavily as the iconic percussion for the song begins. Locke hits every beat as if he's performed the song a million times, and I suppose he might have. Locke's the oldest member of the group and he has the most experience and the most ego, at least in my opinion. Jackson laughs at me and says that Locke is one of the humblest musicians he knows, especially given his years of experience and talent, but I beg to differ.

Locke and I have been in a dozen arguments in the last year alone, even though I suppose he's gotten better in the past couple of months. He's even given me a compliment before the show, which might be the most shocking thing that's happened all year, despite me being able to pull off a nationwide tour with just our cover charges and tips over the past two years.

Jackson is so lucky I'm able to save without sacrificing the equipment and venues that the band needs because I know what's important and I've done my research. Especially given his impulsive nature when it comes to things like money (and women, but that's a different story). The more successful the band is, the more stability Jackson and I have, and the happier he is, the happier I am. That's how it's always been: me and Jack against the world.

Thing is, Jackson is the only family I have, and by extension, I guess the Spades are my family, too. Even Locke. I suppose.

Still standing close to the edge of the stage, not thinking much about it, I glance over at him, since he is in my thoughts. Locke is almost always focused on his drum set or his drumsticks, lost in the music.

Tonight, however, he's looking out at the crowd, and I happen to meet his eyes while he's waiting for his next part.

For as much as I want to deny it and push it away, Locke is probably the most attractive of all the members, at least to me. Everyone has a type, you see, and unfortunately, mine is the grungy bad boy. There might as well be a picture of Locke Kincaid underneath that phrase in the dictionary.

Locke is currently wearing a black sleeveless shirt since he's taken off his trademark black leather jacket and thrown it behind him halfway through the first song, and even with the dim lights of the club, I can see the veins of his forearms as he twists the sticks, the way his biceps bulge just slightly.

He pushes his hair back from his face, sweating under the lights since they're almost halfway through their set, the break is minutes away, and instead of the polite nod I expect, he gives me a crooked half-smile, and unlike with Axel, I am unable to recover as easily. Locke is my type in a way that Axel is not, that's all.

Surprised, I stumble sideways into the groupie blonde who's too busy staring at Axel to even react, spilling part of my martini down my dress and huffing out a frustrated breath.

I could *swear* Locke is laughing as I head to the bathroom to clean up, but of course, I'll never be able to prove it. He's been acting weird tonight, and I make a mental note to tell Jackson never to let him take shots before a set again.

Locke Kincaid is gonna be the bane of my existence, even on this tour, I just *know* it.

Chapter 3

Locke

At the break of our set, while I'm still smiling at Gemma spilling her martini, Axel is looking around the crowd.

I stand up and rub my face with the hand towel I keep on stage, being careful not to snag my silver nose ring. It's not as if it's new, I've had it for nearly ten years, but I've made that mistake before and it's not pretty on stage.

"That blonde is waiting for you at the bar, Ax, don't worry," I joke, and Axel shoots me a grin.

"Not looking for her," he says mysteriously, and I shrug.

I don't ask questions about what the other members get up to when the set is over. It's none of my business, as long as they don't get physically hurt. If they wanna roll the dice on getting their hearts broken, that's on them.

I've done my fair share of rolling the dice in that area, myself.

I don't worry too much about Axel, or even Jackson, for that matter. They've been around the block. Axel seems to get a new girl every night, and Jackson has a girl every few months and seems to get over it quickly and move on to the next.

I worry a little about Sam, just because he's so young. Twenty-five might not seem that young to most people, but since I'm in my thirties, it's very young to me. I remember what I was like at his age, idealistic, just *knowing* that I'd somehow make a living off my musical talent alone and meet the perfect woman.

I don't want sweet Sam to have to go through the same things I did, so I admit that I keep an eye on him. Not the way that Jackson keeps an eye on Gemma, of course, but I do tend to watch out for some of the groupies that have a thing for bassists and keep them off his trail.

It's not that I'm celibate or anything like that, God forbid. I've been in quite a few compromising positions, especially since there's a certain type of woman who tends to go after the drummer instead of one of the more out-there members of the band. They tend to be a bit more...aggressive, and it's fun to play dumb until we're behind closed doors. Turning the tables is one of my specialties, I suppose.

Being a rocker has its perks, even if you're still performing in bars and clubs.

Gemma comes out of the bathroom and since her dress is black, the martini didn't ruin it or even make a stain, and I'm grateful. She'd be *really* mad instead of just annoyed, and since everyone is in such a jovial mood, I wouldn't want to ruin things by getting in a real fight with our manager.

I expect her to ignore me. Instead, she stalks right up to me. I'm tall, but in her stilettos, Gemma is *almost* eye to eye with me and her chin is tilted up.

"What's up with you, Kincaid?" Gemma demands to know, and I fight a smile, blinking innocently at her instead.

"I don't know what you mean, little bit."

13

"Don't call me that," she mutters and brushes past me, bumping my shoulder as she heads to the bar.

I've never exactly been the type to like to rile others up or tease people, but something about Gemma makes me want to make her pale green eyes flash at me. It's not because she's younger than me, or because she's my best friend's younger sister. God knows I have zero brotherly feelings toward her, even if maybe I should.

The way she reacts to me is just... more intriguing than those women who come on to me just because I'm in a band.

More intriguing and a lot scarier, especially given that Jackson was staring daggers at me as I thought about his sister.

I clear my throat and make my way to the bar, on the other end of where Gemma is standing, no doubt ordering another filthy martini.

"You better not be doing what I think you're doing," Jackson says, his tone eerily nonchalant as he orders two shots of tequila for us despite knowing my distaste for liquor during our set.

I take in a deep breath.

"No idea what you're talking about, Jacks." I take the shot without hesitation, avoiding the urge to look for Gemma at the other end of the bar.

"I've got enough to worry about on this tour that I don't need you *and* Axel making eyes at my baby sister," Jackson grumbles, taking only half his shot, which is almost as unusual as what he's saying.

I begin to nod and then my eyes widen and I look over at Jackson.

"Axel? The tour?" My head is spinning and I doubt it's from the alcohol. "Gemma's not coming with us." It isn't a question. There is no possible way that Gemma Arden is coming on tour with us. What's she gonna do, sleep on the tour bus with a bunch of guys? "And what the hell does Axel have to do with Gemma?"

"You haven't noticed him winking at her onstage and showing off his stupid sleeve?" Jackson huffs. "I've been on the defensive, keeping him away from her since sometime last year. What are you, blind?"

I blink, something feeling tight in the pit of my stomach. Maybe that last shot of tequila was a bad idea after all. And I may not be *blind*, but definitely wrapped up in my own thoughts in the past year – especially when it came to Gemma and the future of the group. For some reason, I find it hard to think about Axel coming on to Gemma, even though I'd already come to terms with the fact that I had zero brotherly feelings toward her. I guess maybe I'm a little protective, nonetheless, on Jackson's behalf. Honestly, I don't like the way I'm feeling as I think about it, so I focus on something else, the other important matter at hand.

"Gemma isn't coming with us," I repeat, staring straight at Jackson.

Jackson frowns. "Of course she is. She's our *manager*, how many times does she have to prove that to you? She's the reason we're going on this tour in the first place."

"But–she has to...she can't-" I find myself stuttering, trying to think of a solid reason for Gemma not to go on the tour with us. A reason other than I am finding it harder and harder not to flirt with my best friend's younger sister, that is.

"Don't have a stroke, Locke," Jackson says with a laugh, clapping a hand on my shoulder. "Maybe I read you wrong. You know I get a little touchy when it comes to Gem. I'm glad that you guys are getting along."

I signal the bartender for another shot even though I know that it might make it a lot harder to stay on beat.

"How long is this tour again?"

"Twelve weeks."

I choke on my tequila and the bartender graciously slips me a plastic cup of water. I smile at her and she winks in my direction – at least a possible distraction from Gemma Arden stuck on a tour bus in close proximity to me for three whole months.

Jesus Christ.

Two hours go by in a blur. That's concerning, really. I'm not usually one to drink during sets, but of course, after the show is over, the bar owner bought us all congratulatory shots, and I don't exactly remember talking up the blonde bartender with the red skirt on.

The next thing I know, the bartender's legs are wrapped around my waist in the bar bathroom, and it doesn't occur to me to be bothered that we're outside the stall because my mouth is on her throat and the music is drowning out the way she's gasping into my ear.

I guess it doesn't occur to me *which* bathroom we're in either, because when a woman's screech and then laugh sound to the left of me, I don't think much of it, until I look over into Gemma's pale green eyes.

Her smile fades and I have to blame what I do next on the tequila because I'm not normally one for public... displays of affection, preferring to save my skills behind closed doors.

As I said, though, Gemma Arden inspires something different in me. So, when her eyes widen but she doesn't leave the room, I just shoot her a grin and hitch the bartender's legs up further, lapping my tongue from her collarbone to behind her ear never taking my eyes of Gemma.

Gemma's mouth opens as if she's going to say something, but instead, it snaps closed and she leaves the room as if nothing happened.

Chapter 4

Gemma

When Locke Kincaid joined the band, I knew he would be a problem. I had been their manager for about a year by then and he had a chip on his shoulder because he was older and more experienced and he didn't like that I was the one that Jackson went to for advice about venues.

But Locke wasn't a front man like Jackson or social media savvy like me. He was a bit of a wallflower, for the most part, although I'd heard some stories from the rest of the guys about how he had a certain way with women.

I wouldn't put it past him to be a bit of a womanizer - with those soulful brown eyes and crooked grin, not to mention the fact that he's tall and broad-shouldered - I shake my head outside the bathroom door, trying not to think about Locke anymore.

The whole reason I'm even thinking about him now is because I didn't realize that he'd be *this* type of problem. The way he'd looked right *at me* while he licked that bartender's neck...

I take in a deep breath and burst out the back doors into

the fresh air. I don't drink much while I'm working, so it isn't the alcohol that's making my head spin. I know that much. It's not as if I'm jealous or anything, after all, I've never considered Locke as anything but a thorn in my side. Of course, I find him attractive, but I also find Axel and Samuel attractive. I'm a hot-blooded American female, after all, and I'm around musicians constantly and have been since I was barely eighteen.

I'd fielded my fair share of offers, and I'd gotten to a few bases before Jackson inevitably ruined everything. My brother told me from a young age that rockers couldn't be trusted, and when I asked if that included him, he hadn't thought that was very funny. Jackson wasn't exactly a Casanova but he had his fair share of flings when we were teenagers. I don't see much of it now, but I'm sure there's a girl or two that rotates through his apartment that I don't know about.

Axel has a different girl on his arm every night, so I've never expected to *trust* any of the musicians that I've been around in the last few years, but hell, don't I deserve to have a life?

I'll be twenty-two years old in a few months and I'm still a virgin, and honestly, it's starting to bum me out a little. It's not that I'm just *that* attracted to Locke Kincaid, right? I'm just sexually frustrated. Anyone would be, being around all these attractive men and being nearly celibate.

Hell, I haven't even been kissed in almost a year, so of *course*, I'm more affected than usual. Plus, Locke has never been flirty with me. He is Jackson's best friend, after all, and so I am even more off-limits than I would be to another member.

What the hell kind of tequila does this bar serve to have him acting like this?

19

Luckily for me, the rest of the boys have already dispersed to wherever they are going and whatever trouble they are getting in, and the payment's done and the show's over, all the equipment loaded into the van that I'll drive back to my place: usually, because I'm the only one sober.

I sit in the van for a long moment before starting it up, thinking of Locke's intense brown eyes. *It's not him,* I tell myself. *It's not him, it's just that you're becoming an old maid, Gem.*

Jackson doesn't realize that he really doesn't have to worry so much. I'm not interested in falling for a musician and being like one of those groupies who follow them around making heart eyes and ignoring all other guys. I'm not interested in a relationship, *period*. I just want to have a little fun.

A girl's got needs, after all.

Every time I've gotten close, my brother has butted in, either just watching me like a hawk or intimidating the hell out of the poor guy until he leaves me alone. I can't believe no one has stood up to him, or at least tried sneaking around with me.

I find myself pouting in the van and I laugh at myself a little as I back out and head to my apartment. *Chin up,* I tell myself. *You've got a plan.*

Not just a plan. I have a front-row ticket to Jack and the Spades' first national tour, and a million chances to finally find someone that my brother can't intimidate. Failing that, Jackson will be busy.

I'll just have to keep it a secret, won't I?

Chapter 5

Locke

Two weeks pass by in a blink, and it's time to start the tour - first stop, Albuquerque. New Mexico isn't high on my bucket list of travel destinations, but I'm nervous nonetheless. Not just because it's the first out of state performance that Jack and the Spades will perform, but because I'll be jammed in next to Gemma Arden for six hours on a tour bus.

A *small* tour bus.

I stand there, staring at it with a frown, until Axel claps a hand on my shoulder.

"You afraid you can't fold your big ass in there?" he jokes, grinning as he boards the bus.

My frown grows wider. Ever since Jackson suggested that Axel's interest in Gemma goes beyond the brotherly affection I assumed every other member felt for her, I've been a little touchy around the guitarist.

Axel, for his part, acts exactly the same as he always does - annoyingly cheerful and bright. It isn't as if I dislike people with positive personalities, hell, I suppose that Gemma has one of those, too. It's just that I don't have that

21

type of personality, and sometimes it can feel like I'm some kind of buzzkill.

Usually, though, Axel doesn't get under my skin. In fact, usually Axel talks me into smiling, makes me laugh at something even when everything seems to be going wrong on stage. I guess I have to admit to myself that maybe the reason I feel so irritated now is because Axel might be interested in Gemma.

What does that mean, exactly? It's not as if Jackson will ever take his eyes off Axel long enough for him to make a move on Gemma, even on tour. Even if he *did*, I'm not sure that Axel is Gemma's type.

But why did any of that matter to me, anyway? I have come to terms with the fact that I'm attracted to my best friend's baby sister, but I don't intend to *do* anything about it. Do I?

I'm still standing outside the tour bus when a wave of disjointed memory washes over me: locking eyes with Gemma, licking that blonde bartender's neck as I wanted to lick her...

Shit.

My thoughts stop there, thankfully, because Jackson kicks me in the ass with a black combat boot and I nearly fall over.

"Get it together, Kincaid!" he teases, his tone just as bright and cheerful as Axel's. "We've got a show to put on."

"Yeah, six hours away," I deadpan, righting myself and ducking to step on the bus. We were supposed to meet at 6:30, but I slept in and didn't make it until nearly 9:00. Luckily, we all indulged a little too much yesterday, celebrating the tour, so as I screeched into the parking lot, I saw Axel and Jackson pulling up in Axel's beat up Honda.

Gemma is considerably pissed, especially since the

show starts in less than ten hours so we won't have much time to set up.

She's already on the tour bus, and I expected her to be glaring at me the second I stepped foot on the bus, but instead, she's turned toward Axel, laughing, her green eyes sparkling. Something twists in my gut, and I blame it on too much tequila last night and no breakfast in my stomach.

I sit down across from Axel, and he gives me a look, as if we're in on some inside joke and it makes me want to hit him. Maybe I'm just hungover and sleep deprived, but it seems like everything Axel is doing is driving me up the wall.

Samuel scoots over a seat to sit next to me and smiles. "Everyone's so excited," he whispers, "but I'm kind of shitting my pants."

His low tone and serious delivery surprise me into a laugh, and I bump into him with my shoulder gently.

"Don't worry, Sammy. We're gonna blow Albuquerque away."

Seven hours later, bleary eyed since I've slept the last four hours, I don't feel so confident, stumbling down the tour bus stairs after Gemma. I nearly knock her over when I miss the last step in my sleepy haze.

"Don't tell me you got into Axel's mobile liquor cabinet," Gemma says, but her tone isn't irritated.

She seems upbeat rather than annoyed, and again I think about how her base personality seems positive – it's just that she doesn't like me. Maybe that's why I'm feeling so odd about Axel, even if I know his interest is purely physical and will go nowhere. I never considered myself a person that wants to be liked, but since Gemma is going to be our manager for the conceivable future (and if I'm honest, does a pretty great job at it), it must be professional jealousy.

Gemma and Axel are always pretty friendly, when I think about it.

I don't realize that I haven't responded to Gemma until she puts her hand on my shoulder.

"Seriously, Locke, you didn't, right?"

She seems concerned, her head tilted up to look into my eyes, and my heart skips a beat.

"Of course not," I mumble.

It comes out gruffer than I intend it to, and her face changes, something like anger or hurt flashing across it. Usually it would make me smile, being able to rile her, but today, after watching her chat with Axel for hours, I want to backtrack so that she doesn't take my words the wrong way.

"Sorry I asked," she shoots back, and I curse myself.

Too late.

She turns on her heel (or well, her Keds, since she's not wearing her heels, at least not yet) and instinctively, I grab her arm.

She whirls around, glaring at me, and I let her go, clearing my throat.

"I just wanted to say...wanted to..." I stumble over my words, not sure what I'm going to say exactly or why I stopped her from walking into the hotel.

Everyone else has already gone inside, leaving the equipment in the bus since we're heading right over after everyone showers and gets ready for the show, so Gemma and I are standing in the parking lot with the sun beating down on us. Albuquerque seems a lot hotter than Tucson suddenly, and I realize that I'm sweating.

"Sorry," I finally say, my words clearer than before since my head feels clearer, more awake. "I'm just tired."

"Tired is rocker code for hungover," Gemma says flatly,

but she favors me with a smile that I return instantly, feeling relief wash over me.

For a second, I think she's going to take my hand and lead me inside, but Jackson comes to the door of the hotel.

"Gem, the reservations are in your name and they don't believe I'm your brother!"

Jackson's yell seems to reverberate across the parking lot and Gemma turns slightly red before she bolts toward the door, jogging slightly.

I stand there for another moment, trying to get my head clear. I guess I must be a lot more hungover than I thought because I blatantly stare at her ass, the way it jiggles in her yoga shorts.

Jackson doesn't notice, and I get to keep my eyeballs in my head.

No more tequila, I tell myself, and that's a promise I swear I'll keep - at least until we get to Vegas.

Chapter 6

Gemma

Locke Kincaid has never been the most normal person I know. He often confuses me, especially because for the past two years, he's largely ignored me or been actively argumentative. There are always moments, though, where he acts normal, as if we're colleagues or friends instead of...whatever we are. Acquaintances? Unfriendly coworkers?

For example, a couple times after a good show he would buy me a shot or give me a compliment on how I'd handled something, and I would be baffled by it for a few days, until he went back to the way he had always been: argumentative and negative.

I figure that's just how he is, the old man of the group, grumpy and jaded. Sometimes, though, something else seems to shine through, and I wonder what happened in his past to make him the way he is now. I'll see him laughing with Jackson or jamming out with Axel during practice or giving advice to Samuel and he seems almost jovial, the complete opposite of the man I had always thought he was.

Since I announced the tour, those moments seem to be happening more and more.

I'm standing outside the elevator with Jackson and Samuel while Axel and Locke sign for their rooms, waiting for the elevator to come down from the top floor, and remembering the way Locke apologized to me in the parking lot.

Had Locke Kincaid ever apologized to me before?

"Definitely not," I mutter, and I don't realize I've said it out loud until Jackson calls my name. I blink and look over at him and he's looking at me as if I've grown a second head.

"What?"

"You're super spaced out right now, did you take a Xanax for the trip?"

"Of course I didn't!" I snap, and it comes out harsher than I'd intended.

"Watch the attitude," Jackson warns, and I instantly snap my mouth closed. Then my brother sighs. "Sorry, kiddo. It's just that I know you have that prescription and you used to take one before flights when we were younger. I shouldn't have asked. You're not a little girl anymore, you can handle yourself."

"No, it's okay. I *did* have an attitude." I laugh a little when he cracks a smile. "I'm just tired; I couldn't sleep on the bus."

"Because Axel was talking your ear off?" Jackson asks dryly, raising an eyebrow, and I shake my head.

"Don't start. I can handle Axel."

Jackson hums in the back of his throat and I know that's a subject that I shouldn't broach right now, especially with emotions running high before our first tour concert.

Samuel shifts, bumping his luggage so that it falls over and then cursing, then apologizing for cursing.

I smile at him, his clumsiness cutting the tension in the air.

I'm thankful when the elevator door beeps and opens, and even more thankful when Jackson lets the doors shut as Axel and Locke come running toward the elevators.

I giggle at Locke's annoyed expression and Axel slowly raising his middle finger up at Jackson, who just stands there grinning at them as the doors close.

"You snooze, you lose," Jackson says simply, and I dissolve into laughter again as my brother watches me curiously.

"Tired," I explain again, and Jackson nods, seeming to take that at face value. After all, I'd always been the type of person to get a bit delirious with lack of sleep, laughing at every little thing and losing motor function as if I'm tipsy, and it's been almost 30 hours since I've gotten a good night's sleep.

I'm not being fully honest with my older brother, though, and I'm too tired to deny that even to myself. I feel strange, as if things are changing in a big way.

Despite the way Locke had looked at me the other night in that club bathroom, I'm under no illusions that he's interested in me in that way. He just likes to shake me up, and he'd done that in spades.

In spades, I think to myself, and manage to choke back another laugh at the pun.

"You *really* have to catch a nap before the show," Jackson says, and I nod enthusiastically, keeping my mouth shut to keep the giggles at bay.

I don't think I'll be able to fall asleep, but as soon as Jackson rolls my luggage inside, I plop down on the bed. I start to drift off before he even leaves. The last thing I hear is the door closing softly behind him.

* * *

There's a knock at the door and it jolts me out of sleep. I rush to the door but it seems like I'm moving slow, my limbs heavy. I have no idea what time it is, but somehow, I don't care. I'm not worried about getting to the venue or about whether or not the guys have woken up to their alarms, or anxious about what might happen the rest of the tour.

As I swing open the door, I feel a smile spreading across my face and heat low in my abdomen. It's familiar, after all it's not the first time I've felt something like lust, but the face of the man standing outside my door is blurred. He's tall, I can see that, but most men are taller than me since I'm not much taller than average. Well built, but that doesn't give me any clues, either. I squint and step forward and the second I do, the man's arms go around my waist, locking at my lower back to pull me close to him and I let out a little gasp.

"Gemma," he says, his voice low, and his face slowly comes into focus as I look up at him. Locke Kincaid's deep brown eyes have something almost feral in them as his face gets closer to mine, and then he stops and opens his mouth as if to tell me something terribly important.

Instead of words, a loud, annoying beep comes out of his mouth, over and over, and I open my eyes, grabbing instinctively for my phone which has vibrated off the side table and onto the floor.

As I root around for it under the bed, my heart is racing just like it was in my dream. As soon as I get the alarm turned off, I sit up in bed and cup my face in my hands, my cheeks hot to the touch.

"What the *fuck*?" I say out loud, blinking.

Chapter 7

Locke

The Albuquerque show goes off without a hitch, despite all of us being nearly late to our own first concert after oversleeping at the hotel.

We're all bleary eyed and exhausted after the show but we keep up appearances, signing albums that we'd recorded last year and never sold.

I have no idea how many we are selling now, but it seems like a lot, with Gemma sitting at a table in front of the stage with a cash box. She's barely looked at me all night, but I feel oddly comforted that she hasn't much looked at Axel, either, or anyone but Jackson, for that matter.

I'm too tired to question why it matters to me *who* Gemma Arden is looking at, and it's a little relieving not to stress about it.

I don't see Gemma again until hours later, around three in the morning.

I stumble into the elevator without paying much attention, having snuck out early since Axel had talked Jackson into drinking with him after the show. I'm *way* too tired for Axel's constant ordering of shots.

Gemma slumps against the back of the elevator, her head tilted back, head resting against the wall, and since her eyes are closed, I let myself appreciate the long lines of her thighs in the fishnet stockings she is wearing, her muscled calves in her stilettos.

I shake my head to clear it and step into the elevator, too tired to take the stairs and trusting myself to behave.

Gemma opens her eyes and they widen as if she's surprised.

"Locke?"

Her voice sounds as if she thinks she might have fallen asleep and it makes me chuckle a little.

"Sorry to disappoint you, little bit."

Gemma hums in the back of her throat, a habit she no doubt picked up from her brother. The Ardens usually make that noise when they don't know what else to say, but I don't mind a comfortable silence, and since Jackson always tries to fill it, I wait to see if Gemma is the same.

"Not disappointed," Gemma mutters, but that's all she says, so I lean back against the elevator railing next to her.

Our hands touch and I don't bother to pull away and neither does she, and the elevator trip up to the eleventh floor seems longer than it did before, my heart beating a lot faster than it had when I was riding up with Axel earlier.

Gemma is two floors above me and she smiles at me as I step out into the hall, giving me a little wave. I realize that she's had her nails done, a deep crimson red that compliments the auburn in her hair.

"Good night," I say, and Gemma just nods at me before the elevator doors close.

In the shower, I keep rubbing my pinky and ring finger as if Gemma had burned them with her slight touch on the elevator rail.

Exhaustion washes over me in a wave and I'm unable to keep my mind from drifting when I lie down on the overly firm hotel mattress, my eyes slowly closing as I wonder what Gemma would have done if I'd grabbed her hand instead of just brushing it, if I'd brought her knuckles up to my lips.

I wake from a dream that I can't quite remember when my alarm goes off and I groan, chucking my phone off the night-stand. Luckily for my wallet, it's hooked onto the charger and just bumps softly onto the ground instead of shattering against the wall.

This phone is the third I've been through in just a few months, so once my head feels a little clearer, I pick it up and scan through my notifications.

I've got an indecipherable drunk text from Axel and I squint down to see the timestamp: 6:07 AM. Jesus Christ, he's been out all night, I guess, and I figure I should call and see if he needs a ride home.

Axel can take care of himself, but I guess I feel a little responsible for the wellbeing of all the members of the Spades—maybe because I'm the oldest, but more likely just because they've become family to me over the past couple of years. Even Axel, as much as he can irritate me.

Before I call, I see another text, this one from Gemma, and bring the phone closer to my face.

My ex used to tease me and tell me that I needed glasses but was too cool to get them, and I guess, in the end, she's right, because here I am, still squinting to see the text on my phone, even though I've increased the font.

I push that memory away, not wanting to think about Janis this early in the morning—or at all, if I could help it.

Gemma's text lists an itinerary for the rest of the tour in the group chat, noting in bold that there's been a change in order: the next city we'll be performing in is Las Vegas, and I groan.

A *nine-hour* drive on that tour bus? I feel sweaty and gross just thinking about it. There's dead silence in the group chat. I suppose everyone else is still passed out.

I send a thumbs up emoji to signify that I've read the change and call Axel, noting that his contact icon on my phone is a dumb picture of him with his tongue out, holding up just his index and pinky finger in the universal rocker sign.

Axel Jermaine is about the closest to a stereotypical rock star that I've ever worked with, and that includes the time I played drums for Bob Seger and the Silver Bullet Band back in Tucson when they were on tour in 2018. I guess Bob is mellow compared to what he might have been if I'd been old enough to drum for him back in the '70s, but nevertheless, Axel puts him and his band to shame on a regular Tuesday.

Axel answers on the third ring.

"Finally!" His words are slurred just around the edges, so he must be sobering up, thank God. I didn't want him puking on the ride back here.

"Some of us sleep, Ax. You need a ride, yeah?"

"Please, I've been sitting outside this strip club for like three hours now and the cops keep circling around. They probably think I'm a bum."

I sigh and pinch the bridge of my nose between my fingers.

"Axel, please don't antagonize the cops. If you get arrested, Gemma will-"

"Gemma can do whatever she wants to me," Axel answers and maybe he's more drunk than I think.

I open my mouth and then shut it again, taking a breath through my nostrils.

"Send me your location, dumbass. I'll be there as soon as I can."

I hang up without waiting for his response, and despite his inebriation, Axel sends me his location and I make it there within half an hour. I don't have the world's best sense of direction and the GPS signal keeps going out.

I feel a jab of worry when I see Axel standing by himself outside the club, leaning up against the brick. The last time I saw Axel, he was with Jackson, and now he's alone.

They can take care of themselves, I remind myself. But with Jackson, it's a little different.

When I first met Jackson, three years ago, the first ten times we hung out, he was always at least a little drunk. Eventually, he straightened out and only drank after shows instead of daily, but since I know he has a tendency to slip back into the bottle when things are stressful, I can't deny that this trip worries me a little.

Axel whoops when he sees me. Swaying a little on his feet, he hops into the car the hotel kindly let me borrow and I grin at him. There's always a possibility that stress or a broken heart or something else will rattle one of us enough to go off the rails, but I know I can count on Axel to *always* be off the rails, and there's an odd comfort in that.

His head lolls against the back of the Camaro's leather seat as he looks over at me with glassy eyes but with a smile on his face, as always. He smells awful, an odd mix of tequila, cigar smoke, and women's perfume.

"Good thing we don't have a show tonight," Axel comments thickly and I keep the car idling, looking around.

"Where's Jack?" I finally ask when Axel doesn't indicate that we should wait.

"Oh, he went home with a leggy brunette when the club closed at four." Axel's voice sounds extremely nonchalant and it irritates me, especially since Axel was around when Jackson wasn't doing so well.

"Don't you think you should be keeping a better eye on him?"

Axel snorts. "Sorry, *dad*."

I roll my eyes. Axel clearly isn't sober enough to have an adult conversation about this, and even if he were, I don't think I'd get the response I want, not now.

Axel can be surprisingly level-headed when it comes to the band, despite how much he parties, and when I approached him a few months after I joined the band about how Jackson might be spiraling, he'd been instrumental in scheduling a meeting and talking to Jackson. He stopped offering to buy him drinks, kept a good eye on him. We all did.

I guess the difference is that I still do, and Axel seems to have switched places with Jackson from a few years ago—I worry that, behind the scenes, he might be drowning. I know that I can come off as cold, but inwardly, I worry about my friends.

"Everything good with you?" I ask idly, hoping that it sounds nonchalant.

"Five by five," Axel responds, which is his standard response, but he usually only uses it when referring to amps or how his guitar sounds, not anything personal. In fact, lately, Axel doesn't talk about anything personal at all. Not that any of us ever has, really. In a group of guys that are also rock musicians, there isn't a whole lot of talk about feelings.

I'm not so sure everything is five by five with Axel, but he clearly doesn't want to talk about it, closing his eyes and sleeping on the half hour trip back to the hotel. He manages to get to his room on his own, but I follow him up to his floor nonetheless.

He doesn't complain that I'm watching out for him like he usually would - after all, it's not like we're more than a few years apart in age.

Axel stops at the door of his hotel room, grabbing onto the doorjamb as if for support and turning to look at me.

"Thanks, Locke," he says softly, and for a moment, I think I should ask him what's wrong again, find out what's going on, but then he walks inside and shuts the door.

Chapter 8

Gemma

I sleep like a rock on Saturday night, thank God, because if I'd gone another night without sleep, I might have fallen out in the elevator or something. My sleep was also blissfully dreamless that night.

I barely remember seeing Locke, but somehow, I remember the way his hand brushed mine, the way he stood close to me, shoulder to shoulder, in the elevator.

Locke isn't the type to get so close physically. He's not like Axel, who will drape his arm around my shoulders or slip it around my waist when he walks up next to me, or even like Samuel, who will rest his head on my shoulder affectionately. Locke barely ever touches me, even by accident, and while I consider Axel and Samuel friends, I don't exactly feel the same way about Locke.

Most of our conversations are contentious and even the polite ones are strained at best, so Locke's change in attitude confuses me. He's different down to the smallest details, smiling at me when we meet up in the hotel lobby so that we can talk about the itinerary for the rest of the tour.

I smile back briefly and look for my brother, but he's absent.

I look down at my phone and realize that I don't have a text or a call from him, either, so I panic just slightly.

"Uh, has anyone heard from our lead singer? We can't exactly head to Vegas without him."

I attempt to keep my words light, not wanting to accuse anyone even though I know that Axel is the one who invited my brother out for drinks the last night.

Axel looks bleary-eyed but unconcerned. "He'll be here in a minute," he assures me, and I frown.

Sure enough, my brother comes through the front door of the hotel in a rush, his long blond hair sticking up everywhere, his clothes rumpled. He's still wearing the white button-up and black leather pants with combat boots from the concert, and my frown deepens when the smell of liquor wafts off him.

My brother has always taken care of me, don't get me wrong. He's never done anything to make me feel unsafe or unstable. When it comes to me, Jackson is extremely level-headed and (over) protective. In his personal life, though? He's not so down-to-earth.

Jackson has a particular weakness for both liquor and groupies, and instead of being a womanizer like Axel, he's more of a serial monogamist. However, most of the girls who follow the Spades around aren't usually the commitment type.

"Sorry," Jackson mutters, and I want to be angry and scold him but I know it isn't my place. Besides, he's not stumbling or slurring his words, so at least he's slept it off somewhere—likely in some groupie's bed.

I don't have anything against the fans of The Spades, of course. Hell, that's how we're able to go on this tour, how we are able to make a living. Jackson saved twenty grand for me to go to college, and he'd been furious when I refused to enroll—until I took a few classes at a technical college in marketing and business models and began to manage his band.

I took the savings that Jackson had given me from our parents' estate and bought the best equipment, booked the hottest venues, paid for the right ads on social media: Facebook, Instagram, Snapchat. Just managing the social media is a full-time job, really, but I don't think we're in a place yet that I can outsource and hire someone in marketing to do it.

The savings are dwindling, which is why I've saved up our cover charges over the past few months instead of dipping into them. Axel needs a new guitar as it is, and Locke could use a new pair of cymbals. Instruments and record booths for recording are expensive, not to mention the outfits I purchased for them to wear, the amps and other equipment, and the tour bus that I'd rented.

The hotels I reserved are Mariotts and Super 8s, not the Ritz Carlton, but nevertheless, expenses are adding up. Last year, we dropped a pretty penny on recording and producing a mini album, a little more than a demo but less than a full album.

We bought a ton of records, vinyl, because that's what's popular now—we're popular on Soundcloud already and I've even been able to get us onto Spotify, but in terms of physical purchases, vintage is back: vinyl and band t-shirts. I have boxes of the shirts and albums that we hadn't sold, and last night, I managed to sell a ton of them. I feel proud of how well we did and I can't wait to tell everyone, so I keep my mouth shut about my brother, his drinking, and his potential groupie.

"All right, you bunch of hungover buzzkills," I begin

dryly, and Locke cracks a smile even when no one else does. "You guys haven't even asked about sales. Wanna know how many tickets we sold last night?"

"The venue seemed sold out," Samuel comments, and everyone else seems bored or sleepy, so I sigh.

"We did sell out. We only sold half online, so I was worried, but at the door, we ended up with standing room only, and the owners of the venue want us to call them first if we do another tour next year."

Axel whoops and my brother puts two fingers in his mouth to whistle loudly while Samuel applauds me, and I blush slightly. Locke just keeps smiling at me, leaned forward with his elbows resting on his thighs.

"Hold your applause, you guys did all the hard work."

"That's bullshit and you know it," Axel pipes up. Locke raises his eyebrow, glancing over at Axel as if shocked by what he's said. "You do *all* the real work around here, princess."

Locke shifts on the lobby couch, his shoulder stiff and seeming to almost widen as he turns toward Axel. I just watch, curiously at first, a blush heating up my cheeks.

One of my biggest weaknesses is praise, and Axel Jermaine seems to have picked up on that. It's not the first time he's complimented my work or my looks, and every time, my skin heats up and I hope that it doesn't show on my face. Even if I'm not interested in Axel in that way, a handsome man telling me I did a good job makes me blush a little.

Today, it's clear that my expression is obvious, since Axel smirks at me and Locke frowns in my direction.

Locke never likes it much when I receive compliments, I think, and it causes a pang of sadness in my gut. I shouldn't care what Locke Kincaid, or any of the Spades, thinks other than my brother, but I do. Especially Locke, and I can't quite figure out why his opinion matters to me more than the others'.

I suppose it must be because he always seems against me in some way, and honestly, that makes sense.

Before I'd begun managing the band, Locke had been doing the managing, in his own way. It wasn't until I came in and began to change things that we began to argue. I never *want* to argue with Locke, though. It's always him that starts something. Or at least, it used to be him.

Now, Locke doesn't say much of anything, even though I'm surprised that he doesn't argue that Vegas should be on the back end of our tour. I figure I should, at least, bring it up, in case some of the others are thinking the same thing that I assume Locke is thinking.

"So, I know the change from Lubbock to Vegas seems counterproductive," I start, and all four of the Spades just blink at me as if they have no idea what I'm talking about. "We were all expecting Vegas to be our last hurrah and everything, especially with two shows. One is even at Aphrodite's Lounge!"

There might as well be crickets jumping all over the hotel lobby because they're just staring at me blankly.

I look over at Locke, though, and he's the only one who's *not* staring at me, in fact, he's staring down at his lap as if he's got something to say but doesn't want to argue—and that's certainly not like him.

I narrow my eyes at him slightly, trying to will him to look at me, but it doesn't work, so instead, I clear my throat and call his name.

Locke shifts in his seat again like he had when Axel complimented me, and looks up at me with deep brown eyes. He looks oddly conflicted, as if he wants to say some-

41

thing but he also doesn't want to say anything, and it's beginning to stress me out.

"Spit it out, Kincaid," I order, and I don't mean for it to come out that demanding but I see a slight uptick at the corner of Locke's mouth—a smile?

"Well, I was just thinking that with the way the itinerary is now, we're beginning in Albuquerque and ending in Houston, and with no shows on the East coast—it doesn't feel like we really made a national circuit, does it?

I open my mouth and then shut it again. Locke has a good point. I had a hard time finding venues on the east coast, and the itinerary shows that.

"You think we should have a show in Nashville?" I say, mostly joking because Nashville is notoriously hard to book if you're not a country western band.

Locke looks right at me, not breaking eye contact or flinching, still with just that slight upturn of the right side of his mouth, a dimple I'd never noticed before showing in his cheek.

He shrugs. "I know some people, could put in a call..." He pauses and it's such a long pause that I know it has a purpose. "If you want me to."

I take in a deep breath through my nostrils and blow it out through my mouth and his smile becomes more obvious, his dimple deepening. I don't know why I feel so tense, exactly, other than Locke Kincaid seems to have some kind of hold on me. Why do I seek his approval, anyway? I don't care that he's older than me, but maybe it's because he has so much experience with music...

I let out a long sigh.

"Call your guys in Nashville. We can boot Houston and end the tour there."

Locke nods, looking awfully pleased with himself, and it

makes me want to scream just a little. I can't explain why exactly this man gets under my skin in a way no one else does, but there's just something *about* him. It's the way he looks so smug when he finds out he's right in an argument. The way I can tell that he loves making me angry, the way I can tell that he loves making me blush.

There's nothing sexual about it, of course, and hell, maybe that's part of what makes me mad.

At least when Axel flirts with me, even if it riles me up, I know that it's because he does desire me, at least physically. He's made his intentions well known, despite the lies I've told my brother, but with Locke? It's not like he desires me, it's not like he considers me a real rival...

I have no earthly idea why Locke Kincaid likes riling me up, and that's what drives me crazy.

"I would have angled for New York," Axel pipes in, and Locke gives him a sharp look that makes my breath catch in my throat.

Locke Kincaid is a handsome man, that much is undeniable, but he's not *strikingly* handsome, not like Axel or even my brother. Something about Locke's face only strikes me when he's angry or very serious. His jaw tightens at just the right angle, his mouth sets just so. His brown eyes seem to go darker and whatever he's focused on has *all* his focus.

As I watch him glare at Axel, I wonder if Locke looks at women like that, after he's got them half-dressed beneath him. My cheeks instantly flood with heat and I clear my throat again, trying to work my phone out of my back pocket and nearly fumbling it on the ground.

I think I hear a chuckle from Locke but when I look over at him, he's just blinking up at me innocently. Damn his big brown eyes.

I make it a point not to fumble again when I add a note in my calendar to rework the itinerary.

"We have six days to get to Vegas, guys, so we can park the tour bus here and-"

"Absolutely not," Axel demands, standing up. "If we're gonna have downtime during this thing, I want to have it in Vegas, not in *Albuquerque*."

Axel says the city name with such disdain that it makes me giggle, and both Locke *and* Jackson give me a sharp look that makes me clam up immediately.

I'm not *afraid*, mind you, just cautious of my brother's wrath. And not for myself. As for Locke? Frankly, I don't know what the hell I feel about him.

"I don't wanna leave yet," Jackson complains, and Axel grins and shoves at his shoulder playfully.

"Certain pair of long legs?" he cracks, and Jackson grumbles but he's smiling, wonder of all wonders, after what a grump he's been this entire trip.

"We'll take a vote," Samuel suggests, always the level-headed band member, and everyone groans but I smile at him.

I think for a moment, looking over at my brother. I don't know what went on with him and the girl he picked up last night, but he seems to be loath to leave Albuquerque right away, and even if that worries me a little, Jackson deserves a break now and then.

"Good idea, Sam. I'll go first. I vote for a hybrid break— one night here in Albuquerque and then tomorrow morning-" When everyone stares at me as if their souls are leaving their bodies, I pause and sigh. "Fine, tomorrow *afternoon*, we'll leave for Vegas, spending a night in a hotel halfway."

Everyone votes for my idea except for Axel, who keeps

pouting in my general direction, even if not right at me. I don't think he means it, really, because in just a moment, he's on his phone, probably making plans for the night.

Axel certainly isn't the most likely member to hang out in the hotel the whole time. That's more Locke's style.

I guess, anyway. What do I know? Things seem to have changed in the past few days, so I don't know *what* Locke's style is, particularly on this tour.

On the way to the elevators, I expect Locke to hang back, but as if to prove his recent unpredictability, Locke comes up to stand between me and Axel.

Axel makes a noise in the back of his throat and I put my hand to my mouth to cover a smile. I have a suspicion that Axel wants to get me alone, and I'm certainly not against that idea, despite how my brother might feel about it.

To his credit, Axel merely leans over, ignoring the taller man between us, so he can see my face.

"You wanna have a drink later at the hotel bar?" he asks, and I open my mouth to speak but Locke speaks first.

"Sure," he says, his tone uncharacteristically cheerful.

Samuel and Jackson have walked up behind us, also waiting for the elevators.

"What time?" Samuel asks.

Axel sighs deeply. It's a little dramatic and it makes me want to giggle. Again. I guess last night I didn't sleep enough to get me totally back on my game. All this giggling is not normal.

"How about eight?" Jackson says, coming up behind Axel.

"Great," Axel says flatly, and I suppress the urge to laugh again.

Chapter 9

Locke

Jackson seems too tired and hungover to pay attention to what Axel is saying to Gemma, or to how she reaches across the elevator to wrap her fingers around his forearm, but *I'm* watching in his stead. Jackson clearly has a new girl that he's interested in, because that's the only time he gets like this—quiet, focused on something that isn't his sister, having fun or music.

It's bad timing, for sure, given the tour, but we've got some down time and clearly another night in Albuquerque pleases Jackson, because he's humming as he goes into his room, telling us that he'll meet us at the hotel bar at eight.

I'm not sure that he will, given that Jackson tends to get wrapped up in relationships, even when they're brand new —*especially* when they're brand new. Between Jackson and the strange way Axel acted the other night, I find myself worried about the rest of the tour, especially Vegas.

What I refuse to worry about is how it feels to see Gemma's manicured nails digging into Axel's tattoo, the way he raises his eyebrow at her. I'm gonna pass off what- ever weird territorial thing I have going on with Gemma as

46

worry for Jackson and what he will think of Axel getting his paws on her.

Samuel and I are on the same floor, so we come down to the bar together, and for a moment, I think that we're early. I look down at my phone and it's fifteen past the hour, fashionably late, of course, as rockers should be, but then I see Gemma's long, auburn curls bouncing as she throws her hair over her shoulder and I try not to glare at how Axel leans closer to her on his bar stool.

Why is she dressed like that? I think, and then, like an idiot that has no filter, I hear myself saying it out loud as Samuel and I approach the bar.

Gemma turns to look at me, her smile fading, and she looks me up and down.

"Why are *you* dressed like that?"

I look down at myself, wearing a pair of ripped jeans and a black t-shirt and my old black boots.

"I'm always dressed like this," I complain, and Axel bursts out laughing. I wonder how much they've already had to drink because Gemma is smirking, too, her pale green eyes seeming brighter than usual.

"You guys were early," Samuel accuses, but it's lighthearted—a lot more lighthearted than my tone, anyway.

"Just a little," Axel promises.

Gemma nods and signals the bartender for shots. I wrinkle my nose but Samuel shrugs and thanks her.

I refuse mine and Axel takes it instead, tipping it toward Gemma with a wink.

I want to push him off the bar stool.

Instead, I sit down next to Samuel, who's taken the spot next to Gemma. Jackson is, predictably, nowhere to be found.

"So, what do you say, Gem? You're dressed for it, yeah?"

Axel asks, and I make it a *point* to glare at him this time, placing my palms down on the bar.

What I really don't like is how it seems like they had a conversation previously to this meeting.

Gemma proves that theory by what she says next, and something like rage makes my skin feel hot.

"I told you I was down, I just don't want to go to a strip club."

"Strip clubs are *fun*, Gem."

"So then, can we go to a male one?" Gemma teases, and Axel raises an eyebrow, choking on his Patron and pineapple.

Samuel breaks out into laughter, too, and I open my mouth to say something about Jackson, but Samuel surprises me.

"I'll go with you. Keep your brother off your trail," he offers, and I stare at him, my mouth still open.

Gemma gives him a big, open smile, bigger than she'd ever favored me with, that's for sure.

"Thank you, Samuel. You can be my chaperone." She links her arm through his, resting her manicured nails on his bicep, and Samuel blushes deeper than the Bloody Mary I've ordered. Vodka seems a lot more palatable than tequila at this point in the trip.

Especially with Gemma batting her eyes at not just our lead guitarist, but the bassist, too.

If Jackson was here, I think, and then I look over at the three of them, thick as thieves. Axel doesn't seem to mind that Samuel is tagging along, and that bothers me. I think it would have bothered Jackson, too, if he'd bothered to be here.

I knew he was worried about Axel, but Samuel isn't on

his radar as a threat to Gemma, and I believe that Axel feels the same way, which is why he's unconcerned.

"I'm coming too," I announce, and everyone turns to look at me, surprised. "No strip clubs."

"Party pooper," Gemma whines, and Axel gives me a hard look that I return in kind. He's the first to look away, and it gives me an odd sense of satisfaction.

Usually, Axel would be the first to stand up and announce that we should leave now, get there early, before cover starts, but he remains quieter than usual, sipping his drink instead of chugging it, talking and laughing with Gemma.

I'm not great at inserting myself in conversations that don't involve me, but I do my best in this instance, asking Gemma about tour cities and doing my level best to ignore Axel.

Gemma looks at me curiously but she answers my questions easily, chatting with me and Axel in kind without giving either of us too much attention. Gemma's marketing brain stays on even in her social life, it seems, and I find it a little impressive.

I find it difficult to be "on" all the time in that way, but Gemma seems to have perfected it, and I wonder what's under that façade—maybe for the first time since I've known her.

It'd be nice to continue talking to her about the tour and other things, since this is the first real conversation I've had with her that is actually civil and not either teasing or argumentative, but Axel, as I already suspected, has other plans.

"They'll start charging cover, soon," he complains, and Gemma rolls her eyes.

"Tell me you're broke without telling me you're broke."

Axel puts on a wounded expression, clutching at his chest dramatically.

"Talked yourself right out of me paying for your cover, sweetheart," he teases her, and Gemma shrugs.

"That's okay—unlike you, I *have* money."

Samuel snorts out part of his draft beer and has to ask the bartender for a pile of napkins to wipe off his shirt, and while I'm in the midst of helping him, Axel somehow leads Gemma toward the parking lot.

I dab at Samuel's shirt, frowning as I watch them leave, and Samuel slowly takes the napkins from me, watching my face.

"What's going on with you, Locke?"

I shake my head, but I'm still frowning. Gemma has the keys to the tour bus, so it isn't as if we really have a choice what to do next. I grab Samuel and haul him up from the bar, throwing cash at the bartender, who just grumbles at me. I expect that he sees a lot worse than this quartet, but it's probably frustrating, all the same.

I always try to treat bar staff well because they do a lot to market our band, even on their own social media in some cases. The bartender who I'd hooked up with back in Tucson, for example, had been one of our biggest fans, posting our concert dates a week in advance on her Instagram, where she had a fair amount of followers due to her social attitude and good looks.

Tonight, however, we aren't performing and it isn't a *real* bar, just a hotel, so throwing a fair amount of cash and dragging my younger friend out of the place in order to catch up to Axel and Gemma isn't something I'm going to lose any sleep over.

Samuel breaks free as we get to the parking lot, and I've

lost sight of Gemma and Axel. I'm willing to leave him behind, but he calls my name and I stop, sighing.

"Listen, you can't tell Jackson if anything happens with Axel and Gemma," Samuel says quietly, as if not wanting anyone to hear or as if Jackson might be lurking around the corner.

I look at him for a long moment, wondering if there is a vein bulging out of my forehead with how fast the blood rushes to my face at the suggestion of something happening between Axel and Gemma, or the suggestion that Samuel might somehow be *okay* with that.

"Sam, what are you talking about?" I ask, and there must be some warning in my tone because Samuel looks away, down at his hands, before looking back at me.

"Gemma deserves a life, Locke. She deserves to make her own decisions."

"What do you know about what Gemma deserves?" I can feel my shoulders straightening but Samuel doesn't back down.

"A lot more than you and Jackson do," Samuel says, firmly but, as usual, quietly, and I swear I think my eye might be twitching.

It's like the whole world has turned upside down or something.

"All of us protect Gemma," I insist, as if this should be obvious. "That's part of what this band—what this *family*— is about."

"Is it?" Samuel asks, not breaking eye contact like he usually would. "Is that what you're doing, Locke? Protecting Gemma? Or do you just want her for yourself?"

My throat works as I try to think of something to say back to that, but instead, I just turn on my heel and stalk toward the tour bus, and I clamber on board while Samuel runs along after me.

Axel and Gemma are sitting across from each other on the tour bus, Axel's hands hovering over Gemma's bare thighs, and he doesn't even have the decency to move when I board the bus. Luckily for him, Gemma does, clearing her throat and moving to the driver's seat.

"Everybody ready?" She looks around at us while she starts the bus. Samuel smiles and Axel whoops.

I just look at her until she turns away because I don't feel ready at all. For any of this.

Chapter 10

Gemma

It's lucky that I'm driving the tour bus because if I wasn't, I'd probably be stuck sitting between Locke and Axel while they had the world's most obnoxious stare down. I don't look back to see if that's what's happening on the short ride to the club that Axel suggested, but I can just *feel* it. I plan to talk to Samuel and slide him the keys to the bus so that he can drive us back, because God knows I need more to drink, and Samuel never overindulges.

I'd been hoping that my brother wouldn't show up to the hotel bar but I never thought that Locke would show. He isn't the type to show up to social events that aren't pre-planned weeks in advance, and even then, it's fifty-fifty. Locke Kincaid is maybe the least social rocker I've ever met, and so, even though he'd said he would come, I didn't expect it to actually happen.

Why did he show, anyway? Locke isn't a club rat. In fact, most of the reason I was so surprised about him putting on that show in Tucson with the bartender is because it was so out of character. I guess I'm right about him changing his tune, so to speak, because he's chatting away to Samuel and acting like the life of the party, even though he isn't drinking much, even when we get into the club.

I order two shots at the bar and take them both, making Axel raise an eyebrow.

"Gemma gone wild," he stage-whispers in my ear, and I giggle.

Axel makes me giggle a lot, and I'm grateful for his friendship. Hell, I'm even a little grateful for his flirting, because it seems to rile up Locke Kincaid, which is something that delights me for reasons I don't understand.

I decide to make the most of tonight. It is a rare occasion that I can hang out like this, with my friends—male friends—and not have my brother breathe down my neck, or their necks, whichever he feels might work best to ruin my love life. That's why I'm still a virgin. And it's weird enough being a twenty-one-year-old virgin, but even weirder that I didn't *intend* to be a twenty-one-year-old virgin.

I've had boyfriends, of course, ever since high school, but after our parents died, Jackson cracked down on my social life, and I understand why he did it, but now?

I'm a grown woman. I can make my own decisions. And I decided to try to pursue a night with Axel. I don't love him, but I want my first time to be with someone who cherishes me, cares about me, and treats me right. But I'm not looking for forever. I just want to know what it feels like to be worshipped. To be touched by a man. And I know he'll treat me right and our friendship won't change if he helps me with this.

But, even though tonight, my brother isn't here to stop me,

Locke is, and for some reason, he's making it his personal mission to cockblock me.

Even as I take my first two shots back-to-back, with Axel right next to me, hip to hip, Locke manages to wedge himself between us. That's no small feat, given Locke's height and wide shoulders, and I glare up at him.

"Hello," I say icily, but Locke doesn't seem to take the hint, smiling down at me.

"Hello," he repeats, and orders himself a coke.

He orders *a coke*, at the hottest bar in Albuquerque. Granted, it's not like we're at Caesar's Palace in Vegas (*yet*), but still – this is odd behavior, even from him.

All the Spades are drinkers, even Samuel loves a good draft beer and has been known to get tipsy and giggly when we all go out together. Jackson and Axel disappear—usually with a girl—after a few drinks, and Locke usually disappears to go home. Many times, it's ended up just me and Sam, chatting away until we sober up.

That's how we became such close friends—not that the rest of the Spades have even noticed. They don't notice me in general, even Jackson acts like I'm an invisible force propelling the band forward, but that's started to change—first with Samuel, and now with Axel.

And Locke, I suppose, I think as I make a sour face at Locke, yet again, moving in between Axel and me as we trail out onto the dance floor. Locke doesn't even *dance*.

No matter what I do, or where I move, Locke is right next to me, and it's beginning to drive me nuts, especially since he doesn't seem to have anything to say and all he wants to do is glare at Axel. Jackson might as well be here!

Infuriated, I stalk back to the bar to order another shot, even though I've probably had enough. I don't normally get drunk, just tipsy, and when someone slides up next to me, I feel like I'm going to explode.

"Will you *stop following me?*" I snap, and then look over

to see Samuel's shocked face. I sigh. "Not you, Sammy, I thought you were-"

"Locke," he says, and I want to hug him. Samuel seems to know intuitively how I feel, and I think that maybe Jackson was right when he said that Samuel would be the best Spade for me to date. Too bad Samuel and I have zero physical chemistry. That much is clear to everyone. Including Locke, I guess, because he's nowhere to be found when Samuel and I are alone.

"He's being so *weird*, Sam!" I groan, and I can hear the whine in my voice but I don't care.

Samuel takes one of the two shots I've ordered to keep me from drinking too much and I begrudgingly let him. My head is already spinning. I'm probably dehydrated from all this dry heat, so after I take my shot, I order a bottle of water.

"He's just looking out for you," Samuel says, and I give him a look that makes him wince. "Okay, okay, it's more than that. It *is* weird."

"Thank you," I mumble, and look out toward the dance floor. Axel dances idly with some redhead, but he doesn't look like his heart is in it. I wave to him and he grins, but then his smile fades as Locke comes up to talk to him, leading him off the dance floor.

I huff out a breath, blowing my bangs out of my face.

"Gem," Samuel warns, and there must be a certain expression on my face because he looks concerned. "What are you gonna do?"

"Whatever I want," I breathe, and make a split-second decision.

I push past Samuel and stalk to the edge of the dance floor where Axel and Locke are standing. Without so much as looking at Locke, I grab Axel's hand and start to pull him toward the back doors.

If Locke follows us, I don't notice.

Axel laughs, but then, when I turn to look at him after we get outside, his smile fades.

"Gemma?"

"I need to get out of here, can you drive?"

"Uh, no, absolutely not. But I could walk you to your room," he stammers, uncharacteristically nervous when he's usually smooth.

It's blissfully cool outside, or at least *cooler* than the hot club, and the breeze feels nice on my face. I'm more drunk than I thought I was, and I feel off balance, so Axel's offer to walk me makes me feel a bit better.

I loop my arm through Axel's and we start to walk off, but he stumbles off the curb and I go with him, laughing. I close my eyes against the way the world begins to spin, but then Axel pulls away from me and my eyes pop open.

When I look up a bit further, Locke fucking Kincaid is standing next to him, a hand on his shoulder, his jaw tight, his full mouth set in a hard line.

Goddamn it.

I take a couple of steps back, nearly stumbling, and Axel tries to grab my wrist but I shake my head and he drops his hand. I'm not upset with him, not really, but right now, I'm so angry that I don't want anyone touching me, even the person I'd been wanting to touch me all night.

I look directly at Locke, all but ignoring Axel.

"What the hell are you doing?" I demand, knowing that my voice is too loud.

"Trying to keep you out of trouble. You're not exactly making it easy." Locke's voice is a roar in the alley behind the bar and Axel steps back toward the door, not leaving, but getting out of the way of our argument.

I gape at Locke, shocked that he snapped back at me.

"I'm not a fucking teenager! I don't need to be kept out of *trouble*. Maybe I want to get *into* trouble! Have you or Jackson ever considered that?"

"That's what I need to do," Locke mumbles, as if he's speaking to himself instead of me, but his brown eyes are still flashing. "I need to call Jackson."

"Don't you *dare!*" My voice is nearly a screech at this point and I can't think straight between the tequila and the rage that's rising in me. "I'm not a child!"

"Maybe you should stop acting like one, then," Locke says, his voice lower and suddenly cold, and I have the urge to punch him but manage to control myself.

"You're not my father *or* my brother, so how about you mind your own business, Kincaid?"

Finally, it hits me that Axel hasn't said a word, hasn't stood up for me even though he's become my best friend, so my eyes dart to his and he gives me a very weak smile. I narrow my eyes and it fades, just like it had before, and I tell myself I'll never speak to him again.

When I'm sober, that might change, but right now, the only member of the Spades I'm willing to acknowledge is Samuel and I stalk inside to find him.

By the time I find him, my vision is blurring, either from tears or tequila or both. *Men!*

Chapter 11

Locke

Axel is unusually quiet on the way home, and not for the first time, I wonder what's going on with him. It's clearly something. Axel has always been a bit of a party animal but this isn't like him. He doesn't get pensive or maudlin when he drinks. He doesn't do quiet. Yet, here we are. He's not glaring at me or teasing me for cockblocking him like he usually would, and it worries me.

I was so mad at him just an hour ago that I couldn't see straight, but now all I can do is wonder what the hell is going on. Gemma won't even look at me, just gets on the bus with Samuel and heads to the back to lie down, facing away from us and bundling up in a blanket. I suppose that means I'm driving, since even Samuel seems to be pissed at me, crossing his arms over his chest.

I assume that Gemma is asleep when I pull off, but the second I turn off the bus, she stalks down the stairs and stumbles into the hotel. Samuel follows. And when it's just myself and Axel on the bus, I turn to look at him. Instead of laughing or smiling or cracking a joke like he usually would, he just shrugs and heads into the hotel.

I sit in the driver seat, staring out the windshield for several minutes before I go inside. On the elevator, I think about getting off on the eighth floor, since that's where Gemma and Jackson are staying. I tell myself it's because I should tell Jackson what went on. I even hit the button, cursing when I realize that I can't talk to Jackson about it without seeming like I'm tattling on Gemma.

You're not in fucking preschool, I think, but nonetheless, as the elevator doors open when I get there, I just stick my head out the door and look down the hallway, presumably to make sure Gemma or Axel haven't passed out in the hallway. They've both had too much to drink. No one is lying in the middle of the floor, though, so I step back into the elevator and go up to the tenth floor and head to my room.

I know that I should talk to Jackson, but not about Gemma. As strange as I've been feeling lately about Gemma, I honestly don't trust myself to talk to Jackson without revealing something that will make him take my head off. The thing is, I'm bigger than Jackson, but he's broader and he's a dirty fighter. And though it's been a while, I've stopped enough of his brawls to know that he's never ended a fight without blood and bruises, and usually emerged as the winner. I can hold my own, maybe even against Jackson, but if I can avoid a few shots to my pretty face, I will.

Especially since I'm not sure what the hell has put this bug up my ass about Gemma Arden. Even when I learned she was managing the band, I didn't think of her as more than Jackson's little sister. I worried briefly about her ruining things with the band, but overall, I didn't think she could do much damage. Now, it's like I spend nearly every waking moment worrying about her in some way, and what the hell do I have to be worried about anyway?

That she might get laid? The thought sends a shiver up my spine and I rub my hands over my face. That can't be it. *I'm not jealous.*

I mean, I am the jealous type, I even had to rein in that part of myself sometimes, especially since, after Janis, I didn't exactly do real relationships. Once I hooked up with a girl more than a couple of times, I tended to get possessive, especially if we ran in the same circles. Given that a lot of my hookups were women who followed the band around, that happened a lot. I had to ignore the way it made me feel when they'd flirt with another member of the band or some guy in a bar, because at the end of the day, they weren't mine because I couldn't be theirs. I'm not the type to ask for something that I can't give myself, and so far, it's been easy enough to distract myself from my possessive nature.

I'm not feeling possessive over Gemma, even though I find her attractive. I've never touched her and I never *will* touch her, so there's no reason to be possessive. It's nothing to do with that, despite how I've been seeing her as a woman lately, instead of just my best friend's baby sister, despite that night at the bar when I'd teased her with my tongue on that cute little blonde bartender. I'm just worried about her, and not that she might get laid, but that she might get hurt by Axel Jermaine. Axel has never been a one-woman man, flirting with every skirt under the sun. Next to Jackson, he's the member of the Spades with the most fans, just because of his outgoing personality and the way he plays lead guitar.

Gemma, on the other hand... I realize that I don't know that much about her other than what Jackson has told me, but she just seems like a commitment type of girl, with her no-nonsense attitude and the way she didn't take anyone's shit. In fact, it was surprising to see her all over Axel like that, giggling at his stupid lines and putting her hands on his chest, letting him put his hands on her thighs...

I realize I'm fisting my hands and biting the insides of my cheeks when I taste iron on my tongue and I curse. I head to the bathroom to wash out my mouth and splash my face to cool off.

I look up at myself in the mirror, staring into my own eyes, which I've always found a bit disconcerting.

"Get it together, Kincaid," I tell myself softly, and look over at the shower.

My parents never really cared much what I did, as long as it wasn't embarrassing to them. If I dared embarrass them, they would teach me "the hard way" not to do it again, so, I used to do all my embarrassing things behind closed doors, and when you're a hot-blooded teenage boy, that includes a lot of showers. I even joked with Jackson once that the sound of a shower gave me a hard-on after my teenage years and he'd laughed so hard he'd nearly fallen over.

There's a kernel of truth to that, though, and to this day, shower time is still my go to when I need release, because unlike most men,

I don't watch porn, weirdly enough. Not since I started touching, tasting, and feeling women for the first time. Watching it on TV became hollow and unfulfilling, so, eventually, I just stopped.

I figure after the night I've had and the weird way I've been feeling, maybe I need to let off some steam, so I turn on the water as hot as I can stand it. I chuck off my clothes and toss them into the corner of the hotel bathroom.

I haven't gotten laid since that bartender, so naturally the blonde is the first memory that pops to mind when I take myself in hand without much seduction. I remember how small the blonde felt in my arms, her thighs flexing around my waist, the way she went limp when I put my mouth at the base of her throat. That night is still a bit of a blur, after all the tequila I consumed, and to be honest, her face is a little blurry, but I remember how she felt, how her body melted into mine, the weight of her breasts in my hands.

Unbidden, the blonde's hair turns auburn and curly as I slide it through my fingers in my imagination. I just go with it, thinking that maybe this memory has melded into another one, with a redhead this time.

The blonde's body begins to change, becoming curvier in the ass, breasts smaller beneath my palms, and slowly, her face comes into focus in a way I never experienced before— long lashes, pale green eyes...Gemma.

I hear her name as it rips out of my throat in a groan, an ache running from my balls to the tip of my cock, my eyes popping open as I come all over the shower wall.

"Well, fuck," I whisper to myself, chest heaving from the force of my orgasm.

Chapter 12

Gemma

I've never had a real hangover. Mostly because I don't overindulge. I don't like being out of control, and if you drink enough, you'll hit that wall where you begin to forget what happened. Well, I guess there's a first time for everything. I'm sprawled on the bed still in my dress and heels, so obviously, I did overindulge, for once. I try to peel open my eyes, and icepicks immediately stab into my temples.

"Oh Jesus H. Christmas," I mutter a half forgotten saying of my father's, and I slowly stand up, wobbling on my stilettos before I kick them off. Not fun surviving to get to your room, with no memory of how you even got there, only to die from lack of high-heel balance and hitting your head on something. At first, everything is a blur, but slowly, things start to come back to me. My rage at Locke for following me around and not leaving me alone with Axel. My disappointment at my friend, who left me to fend for myself. But mostly the anger at how things went last night.

I stumble to the bathroom to wash my face, groaning

softly when my head pounds with every step. This is why I don't overindulge. The first time I did was in high school with the cheapest wine coolers anyone has ever had. They tasted like sparkling water and I woke up with a very respectable headache, but nothing like this.

I guess tequila is a harsher mistress than white wine spritzers. I groan and drink about a gallon of water from the tap, refilling that stupid paper cup the hotel gives you over and over. After I've had about five of those, I start to feel a little better. Not better enough to consider putting on makeup or looking decent before going downstairs with my luggage. I'm late but no one has called me, oddly enough. I guess everyone must have slept in.

Downstairs, the only people that are waiting are Locke and Samuel, and Locke looks away the second I glance at him. Fine. Not like I want to speak to him, anyway, after the way he acted last night.

I look down at my phone, frowning, and instantly call Jackson. I'm not surprised Axel is as late as me (over an hour), but Jackson usually shows up on time. As the phone starts to ring, I see my brother sprinting through the parking lot and through the front doors, so I hang up, looking up at him.

"What the hell happened to you?" Jackson asks, ever sensitive to my feelings.

"Lovely," I croak, and then put a hand to my throat, surprised at my voice. "Tequila happened to me, what about you?"

Jackson rubs at his right ear and looks away.

"Same. Tequila is a bitch."

I look him over. He looks disheveled enough that he could be hungover, but he doesn't smell like alcohol.

However, I can't get mad that my brother didn't get blackout drunk last night and I nearly did, so I decide to let it go. I let most things go with Jackson, honestly, and not because I don't care. He's done so much for me that I can't bring myself to nag him too much.

Fortunately, I don't have that problem with the rest of the members, so I call Axel on repeat until he tromps down the stairs with his luggage, groaning like a big baby. I'm a little upset with him still, but he gives me a big, open smile, and I can't help but return it.

"Stop vibrating," Samuel grumbles, and when I look over at Locke, he's jiggling his thigh up and down, his hair falling over his face. He blows his bangs back with a huff and stands up.

"Just ready to get the hell out of Albuquerque," Locke replies.

"Amen," Axel says firmly, and we go outside to load up the tour bus.

Locke doesn't speak to me or to anyone else, and Samuel sits beside me instead of next to Locke, which shocks me. I'm also surprised that Axel sits next to me, after last night. I guess he is trying to make amends, or maybe he doesn't even remember what happened at all.

Jackson calls for first shift driving and I'm grateful. I feel a little woozy.

Axel leans down, close to my ear.

"We need greasy hangover food."

I nod so vigorously it makes me dizzy and catch Locke looking at me. When I meet his eyes, he flushes, the sight of it nearly imperceptible on his tan skin.

What the hell is his deal? I think as he looks away. I guess it's anger, but what on earth he could be mad about escapes me. Since Jackson didn't bang on my door at four in the morning, I surmise that Locke hasn't spoken to my brother about the last night.

I start to stand up to ask Jackson to stop for food before we get on the highway, but Axel puts a hand on my thigh to stop me, laughing softly.

"It's okay, doll. I'm more used to hangovers than you are. I'll ask."

It's an oddly gentlemanly thing for Axel to do, and nicer than he's probably ever been to me without me thinking he wants in my pants, so I'm grateful and smile at him.

Samuel leans over the spot that Axel vacates and, apparently I'm privy to all kinds of secrets today, because he whispers in my ear,

"Don't worry. I'll make this happen."

I nod dumbly even though I have no idea what he's talking about. Well, I have some idea. I confessed to Samuel that I am attracted to Axel some time ago, and Samuel has always been supportive of me breaking out of my shell and going for what I want. I guess that's what he means, but I think his promise will be a lot harder to keep than he thinks. Between my brother and Locke fucking Kincaid, I might be cockblocked for the rest of my miserable life.

Waffle House hashbrowns and coffee bring me back to life and I'm even humming as I play slapjack with Axel on the trip. Two hours in, the coffee hits Samuel hard and he all but pushes Jackson out of the driver's seat to pull off into a bathroom.

I'm approaching what I like to call the shadow-realm, which is a place Jackson and I always joke about when I get to the point of exhaustion and sleep deprivation where everything is hilarious and I can't stop giggling. I only managed four hours of reedy sleep last night, induced by my frenemy, tequila. I'm already fighting back laughter as

Samuel sprints into the dirty outdoor stall at the only gas station we could find.

When Samuel sends me a text that says: *Oh my god, I'm stuck, the lock is broken,* I completely lose it and Jackson and Axel laugh with me while Locke stares at me like my face has gone blue, which only makes me laugh harder.

"Somebody help me," Samuel says, his voice thin, through the stall, and I giggle some more, wiping tears from my eyes.

Axel leans down to look under the door, which has only about an eight-inch gap from the ground. "Dude, you're skinny, just wiggle under there."

"The floor is so gross," Samuel whines, and I think I see Locke crack a smile, however slight.

"Sammy, we can't miss the first show in Vegas because you had to take a dump, c'mon," Axel responds and I almost start to giggle again when Samuel sighs deeply, but I manage to keep it together.

At least, until I see Samuel's red face and his shoulders peeking out from beneath the bathroom door, and then I literally cannot take in a breath I'm laughing so hard, falling over onto Axel who's also losing it.

Jackson's filming Samuel while Samuel curses at him, and Locke is...still staring at me, for some reason, which makes me sober up quicker than I expected. When I tilt my head and look curiously at him, he just gives me a slight smile, and since he's been so mad at me, I'm taken by surprise.

We manage to get Samuel out and he complains for another two hours before we stop at a hotel for the night. I'm still smiling when we arrive, but everyone else seems exhausted. I've hit a second (or maybe third) wind and I feel wired and a little loopy.

Locke gets off before me, and oddly, offers his hand to help me step down.

When I take it and smile at him, he blushes very slightly again and something about it makes my heart flutter.

I gotta get some sleep.

Chapter 13

Locke

Okay, so something's wrong. I don't know what it is, exactly, but something weird is happening to me. Maybe I'm getting sick or something, which would be really bad timing given this is our big break and all.

Whatever it is, it makes my face hot and keeps me staring at Gemma Arden. Ever since she broke down in giggles when Samuel got stuck in that gross bathroom, I've had a hard time keeping my eyes off her, and I can't figure out why. I guess I don't ever get to see her laugh much. She's always busy or pissed off at me. But the way she laughed loud and open at first, and then silent, like she could barely breathe, struck me as almost...adorable.

Now, I can't look at her without heat flooding to my cheeks like I'm the blushing virgin I haven't been since I was fifteen years old. I find a lot of women attractive and it's never been like this, so I honestly have no other explanation except that I've been drinking too much and not sleeping enough and I need to take better care of myself.

"The best road trip snacks are hot Cheetos and Snickers

and I don't take criticism," Axel insists. I come into the conversation in the middle, so I have no idea what the others have suggested. It's the second day into the trip to Vegas, and we're all getting a little antsy.

"You're wrong. Zero bars and the blue Takis are obviously the best road trip snacks," I pipe in, and I'm not even sure why I said it.

Gemma's sitting on the floor of the tour bus, which Jackson keeps yelling at her about, but he can't look around all the time, since he's driving, and she's a brat, so she's cross-legged on the floor, playing Solitaire since Axel got way too competitive playing Slapjack. When I talk about my favorite snacks, she whirls around, her green eyes wide.

"You like Zero bars and the blue Takis?"

"Fucking gross," Jackson groans, as if he's long-suffering on this topic.

"Of course, I do. I'm an intellectual," I respond, and I can't help but grin. Judging by her surprise, it finally feels like we're on the same level, instead of me just having a hard time not looking at her or not being strangely angry when she and Axel get close.

Gemma gets up off the floor and sits next to me, as if she's just discovered something amazing.

"Have you ever dipped the blue Takis in that strawberry milk they sell at gas stations?"

I frown. "No, I dip them in the chocolate milk because I'm not a maniac."

Gemma groans dramatically. "God, I thought you really were an intellectual."

I can't help that my frown turns back into a smile and I shrug.

"I guess I could be convinced to try it," I drawl, and the

beaming grin that Gemma gives me makes heat flood to my face again.

A half hour later, Gemma falls asleep against my shoulder, snoring softly. My shoulders feel stiff and I should move away to stretch out, but she doesn't get much sleep, given how we're all heavy snorers, and she looks so peaceful, her angular features softened out in her slumber.

When Axel offers to take her and put her head in his lap, I give him a death stare but he only shrugs and leaves me be. Eventually, she wakes and rubs at her eyes, smiling softly at me. My heart flips over and I have to excuse myself to go to the tiniest bathroom in the world, where I wash my face in the tiniest sink in the world, my shoulders bowed over.

What the hell is wrong with me?

We've got two shows in Vegas, and even though this first one is at a smaller club, it's still a big deal, and I need to be at my best. No more thinking of pale green eyes, auburn hair, and a set of wide hips in the shower. No more staring at Gemma Arden.

I keep the first promise to myself, but the second ends up being a lot harder, especially since Gemma is in the front row at the concert, dancing in a barely-there club dress. Thank God I'm the drummer so I get to sit down in the back, and if I miss one beat, no one will notice over Jackson's raspy vocals and Axel shredding on the guitar.

I manage to avoid her for the most part, which was my plan, but I don't like how Axel keeps winking at her. At this point, I'm a little concerned about Jackson being so distracted that he doesn't notice.

Our lead singer only seems to have eyes for a chubby, cute girl in the second row with bright blue hair, and I want to push Axel off the stage when Gemma whoops his name after a particularly long solo. Part of me feels particularly annoyed since it's a solo that I wrote. I keep my songwriting credits under wraps, giving credit to Axel or Jackson, and they do co-write most of the songs for the group with me.

"Keyed Up," however, was completely written by me, including the melody, and that makes my anger particularly personal, somehow.

It still doesn't make sense to me, the way I am starting to feel protective over Gemma when, previously, I thought Jackson was overprotective, but I'm trying not to think too much about it. Samuel was right, it is none of my business, and I need to do what I've always done when I'm unsure about something: focus on my music.

I do feel petty enough to ask Jackson to credit me for "Keyed Up," though, and when he does the crowd goes unexpectedly wild. I have to admit it's an ego boost, and when we get done with the show, I get bombarded with fans asking me to sign albums.

Usually, Gemma is sitting at a table somewhere near the stage, selling t-shirts and vinyl records, so I can't help but glance over at her in some strange hope that she might be impressed. Instead of Gemma, though, Samuel is in her place, blushing furiously as scantily clad women ask to take selfies with him or for him to sign their skin.

I find this unusual and I'm a little annoyed that Axel also seems to be nowhere to be found, but I know that Jackson will be making the rounds as our charismatic leader, and he won't allow anything untoward to happen. Not that I care, of course. It's not my job to protect Gemma, but I feel better knowing that her brother is looking out for her.

I'm distracted enough that I don't drink too much, like I did that last night in Tucson, and for once, I don't mind the attention and the crowd. I think maybe this is what I needed, and once again my focus on my music pays off with my mood.

Until I realize that the only two members of the Spades who are left at the venue are Samuel and myself.

"Did Jackson hook up with that blue-haired chick?" I ask, wiping my face with a napkin. Being in front of all those lights in the dry heat of Vegas has me sweating profusely.

Samuel shrugs. "I dunno. He took off right after the show."

I hum, finding that surprising but not completely outside of the realm of possibility. I'm beginning to worry about Jackson, as well as Axel, but tonight, I'm trying not to worry about much of anything.

"What about Axel?"

"Who knows? I'm not their keeper," Samuel snaps, and that's surprising, too, even though he's given me some flack for what had happened the other night with Gemma.

It isn't until the next morning, when I get up early for once and start to head down to breakfast, that the most surprising thing of all happens.

Axel and I ended up on the same floor of the small hotel, so as I stand in the elevator, I'm looking toward his room, wondering if he made it home. A girl comes out of his room and shuts the door behind her, her hair hanging over her face, and I appreciate the long line of her thighs for a moment before she lifts her head and I can see her face.

The elevator doors close before she can see me, thank God, because this time, the heat rushing to my face isn't embarrassment at all, but rage.

The woman with the thick thighs I'd been appreciating that just came out of Axel's room at seven in the morning is none other than Gemma Arden.

Chapter 14

Gemma

W ell, last night certainly didn't go the way I expected. As I do the walk of shame from Axel Jermaine's hotel room back down to my own, I miss the elevator and curse. Thank God Jackson is on the first floor while Axel is on the fifth, with my own hotel room being on the third floor. There's no way I'll run into him.

Not that Jackson has any right to be upset about what happened last night—especially since nothing happened.

Safely back in my own hotel room, I decide to take a bath instead of a shower, feeling like I need extra time to think. Sliding down into the hot water, I let out a long breath and allow myself to think about the last night.

Axel and I drank a bit (him more than me, I was still hurting from my friend tequila's betrayal back in Albuquerque), and then snuck out to the hotel. I was definitely too drunk to get back to my room and I'd lost the card key to boot, so Axel offered up the couch in his suite.

Axel had been uncharacteristically quiet in the elevator, though, and it made me nervous. Axel is always talking, so when he's quiet, it usually means something bad. I was too drunk to care too much, though, so I let it go. As soon as I walked in the door, I kicked off my shoes and Axel was staring at me, his blue eyes conflicted.

"Gemma, you know that nothing is going to happen between us tonight, right?"

I scoffed, almost laughing, until I saw how serious his face was.

"Axel, what's wrong?" It seemed uncharacteristic for him to shut down any possible hookup, even me. And even a blind man could see the one-eighty he had done on me. From overtly flirting to complete shutdown in two seconds flat. And I knew he wasn't looking for anything serious with me. I wasn't looking for anything serious myself, which made him perfect for me, so I had harbored some hope that maybe he wouldn't mind helping me with this V-card issue. But looking at him now was like looking at a different man entirely.

"I can't get over her." His hands went to his face and he sat heavily down on the bed. He was looking so defeated.

Turns out Axel's flirting over the last few weeks had been a coping mechanism, a distraction of sorts, and I would have been mad about it, if Axel didn't seem so devastated. We spent the entire night talking about his ex. The silver band around his left ring finger, is actually his wedding ring, and I never knew, because he wears a few others, so it never occurred me to even ask.

Axel and his ex had been married for two years before things went to hell, and he hadn't seen her now in over a year. She refuses to talk to him, but he is not exactly sure why.

We ended up talking all night, and I'd comforted him.

As soon as he passed out on the couch around daylight, I'd made sure he was comfortable and snuck out.

* * *

It sucks that the first night I spend with the opposite sex (even after a night of heavy drinking), is utterly chaste. I sigh deeply, lowering myself further into the hot water. I feel restless, especially after last night. There's something oddly exciting and arousing about sneaking around, and that was never more apparent than last night. My skin still feels hot, but not like it did when I was angry.

Sliding my hand down my throat to one of my breasts, heat bursts in my lower abdomen when my palm skids across my pebbled nipple. I'm no stranger to taking matters into my own hands—pun intended—even if I'm still a virgin in the literal sense of the word. However, I'm usually too busy, especially since the announcement for the tour, for this kind of self-care. In fact, I can't remember the last time I had an orgasm, so it's no wonder I'm feeling antsy. After all, I've been cooped up with all this testosterone for a few weeks now.

As my fingers slide between my lower lips, I close my eyes. I like to fantasize about some muscular, faceless man who will bring me to new heights of pleasure (blame my mother's discarded Harlequin romances), and this time is no different. Fantasy Man has broad shoulders and a narrow waist and I imagine him tossing me on to my hotel bed. I bite my lip when my thumb slides across my clitoris, and the man's face comes into view as I imagine him boxing me in with his strong arms on either side of me.

I see deep brown eyes, a slow smile with a full bottom lip, a long, straight nose with a silver hoop piercing on the left side. It doesn't dawn on me until I'm gasping, my thighs trembling as I dip two fingers inside my entrance, that this is no longer a fantasy man at all, but Locke Kincaid. It's too late to stop, though, I'm vaulted into an orgasm just as I pull my fingers away.

Heat floods my cheeks, and this time, it's embarrassment instead of lust, and I get out of the bath without even washing my hair, which definitely needs it.

"This is all sleep deprivation," I say out loud to myself, and maybe that's part of it, but I'm a lot less giggly and a lot hornier for it to be that. It's not like I don't find Locke attractive, he's a good-looking guy, and his look and style appeal to me. All of the members of the Spades are attractive, though. I'm used to being around male eye-candy, especially in this line of business. And yes, he is my type, to a T, but looks aren't everything. We can barely tolerate each other. I'm sticking to my statement.

While I slip on a pair of denim cut-offs and a tank top, I tell myself the reason that I've been so attracted to Locke is that we've been in much closer quarters lately. It isn't Locke, not exactly, it's just that after the way he acted back in Albuquerque, he's been on my mind.

You went home with Axel last night. Why wasn't it him? My brain supplies, and I huff as I pull my hair, damp at the ends, into a high ponytail.

"Shut up," I say. And yes, I'm talking to myself out loud. It's been a long couple of weeks.

We have the big show tonight at Aphrodite's Cavern, and I need to get some sleep so that I'm not giggly or horny during the show. As much as I've been thinking of punching my v-card, no way in hell I'm letting some stranger in Las Vegas do it.

No shame to women who pick up men in bars—I wish I

had the courage. I just tend to need a bit of connection in order to be attracted to someone, and since Axel has a list of his own relationship problems, I resign myself to staying a virgin, at least until we're back in Tucson.

I slide into the covers fully dressed so that I can sleep right up until it's time to pull on my fishnets and do my makeup for the show. If only...

When I wake up, it feels like I've slept for ten minutes rather than three hours. Hopefully, that's enough to make me act like a normal, functioning human being. I think about yesterday night, how happy and excited everyone seemed, particularly Locke.

The club had been standing-room only and it surprised me that Locke wrote "Keyed Up" because, not only is it the band's most popular original song, but it's my personal favorite, too. I help Jackson with lyrics now and again, and I never even think about asking for credit, so I suppose that's how Locke feels, too. He looked so proud standing around with a group of fans around him, and I can't help but think that kind of passion is hot.

Maybe that's why I've been thinking about him so much lately. This tour has proven to me that Locke truly is in this for the music, and his music is good. Talent is attractive, right? I have no choice but to be somewhat enthralled.

I let out a deep yawn and half-heartedly fix my ponytail and put on my makeup, tugging on fishnets and boots that lace up my calves. Sometimes, it's annoying that I have to dress up for every show, but marketing means you have to put your best face forward, and despite my lack of sleep, I think I do a pretty good job cleaning up nice.

Amazingly, by the time I get down to the lobby, everyone is standing out by the parking garage, fully dressed for the show, as the trip to Aphrodite's Cavern Casino is only about a half hour drive. After spending nearly ten hours on the tour bus, no one complains when they pile on, and I smile brightly at the group of them, feeling proud.

It's sort of strange, being twenty-one and the youngest in a group of rockers, yet feeling sometimes maternal about them, but it's my life, and I wouldn't change it for anything. Singing has always been the thing that Jackson loves more than anything, and I'm so grateful that he's found a family of friends who feel the same way it brings tears to the backs of my eyes. Everyone seems to be in a stellar mood, too, so that makes me perk up.

Well, everyone but Locke.

When I climb on the tour bus, he's sitting all the way at the back on one of the beds, facing the window instead of looking at any of us. That man sure knows how to keep me on my toes. Just last night, he seemed so proud and happy, and now it's like a storm cloud hangs over his head. He does look good, though, his hair slicked back to show his undercut, a new gold nose ring that compliments his skin tone better than the other one. I look away, not willing to have another impromptu fantasy about him.

I sit down next to Axel, who looks a little tired but seems to have more of a spark back in his blue eyes. His face is conflicted when I smile at him.

"About last night..." he starts, and I pat his knee.

"What about it?" I ask, and he gives me such a beautiful smile that I almost have a crush on him all over again.

"Thanks. You really are a gem, you know that?"

Well, that ruins any crush I might have. I yell and hit his shoulder with the heel of my hand.

"No puns using my name! You know the rules!" I yelp, and Axel laughs so hard he nearly falls out of his chair.

Jackson pulls out into traffic just as he does and he

tumbles over on to me. I break into a fit of giggles. Damn it. I guess those three hours of sleep didn't do the trick.

"Knock it off!" Locke barks from the back. "You're acting like a couple of kids."

Jackson turns around to look with a raised eyebrow, but he doesn't comment.

I glare over at Locke. I forgive him for how he acted in Albuquerque just because I guess he was trying to look out for me, in his way, but I refuse to let him treat me like a child for the rest of this tour.

In the end, I let him have his little fit. God knows I've been thinking too much about Locke Kincaid this tour, so I'm going to let it go.

I'm able to do that up until we get to the venue and I'm setting up the merchandise table and the tip jar, along with a sign with our Cashapp and Venmo.

Locke is setting up his drums in the back while everyone else continues to unload the bus, so I look up at him.

"Do you think we should ask the venue to charge cover? They give out the drinks for free–"

Locke cuts me off by kicking something on the stage, maybe a drum, and it makes a sound that reverberates in the venue and makes me flinch.

"Why don't you ask Axel?" His voice is gruff and anger flows over me like a wave.

"What bug is up your ass, Kincaid? I just wanted your opinion-" I glare up at him and he's not looking at me, which only makes me angrier.

"Oh, now you want my opinion?" Locke jumps down off the stage, stalking toward me, but I don't back up, holding my head up. "You didn't want to listen when I tried to tell you not to fuck with Axel, so don't come crying to me now."

"Who's crying?" I shoot back. "I had a wonderful time."

I don't even know what the hell he's talking about, but I definitely don't intend to back down.

Locke sets his jaw in a hard line and stalks past me to the bar, which already has dozens of people standing around. Open bars attract a big crowd, and that's what I'm counting on for the concert.

I breathe deep through my nostrils to keep from screaming in frustration. *What in the hell is his problem?*

The next time I glance over at him is when Jackson and Samuel are calling him over for sound check and there are four empty shot glasses on the bar counter. Locke is a big guy but he doesn't drink that much, usually, so I scoff and look over at Jackson.

Jackson just shrugs, and I understand why he's not too concerned. Jackson himself has performed shit-faced, especially in the early days of his last breakup, so he isn't one to judge.

I'm not either, usually, but I'm tired of Locke judging me when he has never even taken the time to get to know me.

Whatever is going on with Locke is none of my business, so when he misses his cue twice, I don't even blink. In fact, I don't even watch the show, just listen to it while I'm sitting at the merchandise table, occasionally answering yelled questions from people who have never seen the Spades before and selling a t-shirt here and there. Most of the crowd will come after the concert is over, but since Aphrodite's Lounge is a popular casino, I didn't want to miss out on sales. Plus, I can barely stand to look at Locke right now, I'm so mad at him.

It's Jackson's job to make sure the band stays on beat. My job is to market the Spades and make sure people show up, and I've managed almost a full house already. The open bar might have a little to do with it, but people are rocking out near the stage with their mojitos and martinis, so I'm happy. As happy as I can be given that I'm still nearly shaking with anger.

I like to get everything out in the open, instead of letting unresolved emotions fester, so this thing with Locke is really bothering me. I don't know why he dislikes me so much but is also protective of me when it comes to Axel. It's like he thinks I'm stupid, or still a teenager, and I'm nearly vibrating with all the things left unsaid. As much as I want to confront Locke, I also don't want to let him know that he affects me. I keep telling myself that it doesn't matter what Locke Kincaid thinks, but some part of me wants him to understand that I'm a grown woman and whatever I do outside of managing this group is none of his damn business.

Luckily, there's a swarm of people asking questions about the group and buying records and merchandise (mostly t-shirts and keychains), so I'm distracted from my rage for a couple of hours. When I finally make it to the bar, they've run out of mint for mojitos and I sigh dramatically, smiling at the bartender.

"I guess a margarita will have to do. Tequila is a cruel mistress," I quip.

"She is. We go way back," someone says right at my ear, and I turn to see Axel standing beside me, already a few shots in, from what I can tell.

I smile at him. Axel and I becoming even closer friends is a big plus of this tour. I'm getting closer to all the guys, except for maybe Locke. The Spades are the only family

Jackson and I have. That's part of the reason Locke acting this way makes me so upset.

I think that Axel confessing his issues to me must make him feel better, because he's in a jovial mood, flirting with the bartender and sliding me shots left and right. I drink more than I should, but I'm having fun, unlike the other night.

The world goes a little topsy-turvy and I hope I won't have my second real hangover tomorrow. But this is Las Vegas, party capital of the world. If there's ever been a time to go wild, it's now. And since Axel and I are totally platonic at this point, there's no nerves about what might happen.

What happens in Vegas, stays in Vegas, right?

Chapter 15

Locke

I miss two different cues, and I *never* miss cues, but frankly, I'm pissed off and a little drunk. Okay, maybe pretty drunk. The concert goes by in a blur and I don't even care when "Keyed Up" is the last song and everyone cheers so loud it hurts my eardrums.

I can only stare at the back of Gemma's head and wonder why I'm so fucking angry. She's not my little sister, that much was proven the second I started to watch her ass as she walked away or appreciate how long her legs seemed in those little skirts she always wears. I'm loyal to Jackson. Hell, he's my best friend. But at the end of the day, his hang-ups about protecting his baby sister are his own.

I drank enough tequila before the show to be a little honest with myself—I am jealous, but the reasons why escape me. Is it because I wish I'd gotten to her first? That's not like me, I don't lay a claim on a woman just because I think she's hot.

But is it more than that? The way Gemma got the giggles when she was tired, how her green eyes sparkled when she laughed, how excited she got, bouncing in her seat when I agreed to try blue Takis dipped in strawberry milk: something strange is happening the more time I spend around her.

She's just a kid, I tell myself, but then I remind myself that Axel certainly didn't see her that way and I taste blood in my mouth as I bite the insides of my cheeks.

"Kincaid!" Jackson barks, and I start, looking up at him.

"Show's over," he says in a low voice. "Get your shit together."

Sure enough, Samuel and Axel have fled the stage, allowing the group of roadies we'd hired specifically for the big Vegas show to load the equipment up onto the bus.

I should just let it go. I should just stand up and leave the stage and go back to the hotel room we booked that's connected to the casino. Sleep off this bad mood and the tequila.

"*You* get your shit together," I snap back. "You've been distracted this whole tour, and you were flat during the last two songs."

Jackson's eyes narrow as he sets his jaw. He's clearly angry, and part of me craves it, wants him to hit me so that whatever is rolling around in my gut will stop and I can give in to the physicality of a brawl.

In the end, he doesn't say anything, doesn't throw a punch even when I stand up to my full height and take a step towards him. I don't get what I want and I'm left with all this anger rolling in my stomach, and it's uncomfortable.

Usually, when I'm in a bad mood after a concert, I say my goodbyes and go somewhere I can be alone. Most of the time, I'm in a bad mood because my social battery is drained or I feel down because I didn't drum as well as I could have. I would like to say those are the reasons now, but I've had enough tequila to know that's not the case.

Tequila keeps me honest, and sometimes, it tells me what to do (the Janis debacle was often tequila fueled), and right now it's telling me two things.

1. Drink more tequila.
2. Confront Gemma and Axel.

Somewhere in the back of my head, I know that I could just tell Jackson what happened and he would take care of it, or find a half dozen other ways to handle this situation that don't involve me much at all. I'm not Gemma's protector. I'm not her family. I'm not even really her friend.

The thing about tequila, though, is that all those intellectual, rational thoughts take a backseat to whatever impulse I feel at the moment.

After a double shot of Casamigos (bless Vegas and their mostly free liquor), I catch sight of Axel at the far end of the wrap-around bar. Sure enough, Gemma is sitting to his right, her head thrown back, green eyes sparkling. I swallow hard, tasting the unique flavor of reposado on my tongue, and stride over, tapping her shoulder.

Her smile fades when she turns to me, and that only makes me feel worse.

"Shouldn't we go back?" My words come out lower and slower than I expect, and when Gemma looks up at me, her face fades in and out of focus.

When she stands up, she wobbles on her feet, and I wonder if she's been going shot for shot with Axel. Jackson and Axel are the tanks, and while I can hold my own due to my size, Gemma can't weigh more than a buck-forty soaking wet. I feel myself frowning.

I slowly realize that she responded to me and I didn't answer.

Something like "Go back where?" I think she said, and I

don't know if she's being a smart ass or she really didn't hear me.

I'd planned on confronting Axel instead of Gemma, but now that I'm standing here, I barely even notice his presence, even when he says my name twice.

Without allowing myself to think (which is a lot easier with my blood flowing with tequila), I wrap my fingers around Gemma's right wrist and tug. She stumbles toward me, bracing her left hand on my chest, and her touch makes my breath catch in my throat.

"Can we go outside?" I ask, low, my voice husky, and Gemma blinks those glassy, pale green eyes and nods slowly.

She leans down to whisper something to Axel, who whispers something back and nods. I can't bring myself to let go of her wrist. Her skin feels so soft beneath the pads of my fingers.

"He stays here," I command, but again it comes out quieter and slower.

Gemma huffs out a breath but she doesn't pull her wrist away, and after a couple of false steps trying to find the exit, I drag her past the roulette table and out into the parking lot. It's not the same lot we drove into, because the red tour bus is nowhere to be found, but we're outside and the air feels cool on my forehead. Maybe out here, I can think.

"What is going on with you, Kincaid?"

Her voice seems to come from a tunnel, the tinny sound of the music from the casino fading out as we stand in the parking lot.

"You shouldn't drink so much," I say, and she makes this face like she's just eaten a lemon.

"Don't tell me what to do! Besides, you're more tequila than man right now."

"I just...I want you to be safe." I try to keep my thoughts together but I'm struggling to focus.

"Axel is here to keep me safe."

"Axel," I scoff. "You're never safe with him, Gemma, don't you see that?"

"Why? Because he sees me as a woman instead of Jack's little sister?"

Despite her slurred words, they cut through the fog in my brain.

"That's not what I mean. He'll only break your heart."

Gemma looks confused for a moment before her face hardens again.

"I'm not a sixteen-year-old girl with a crush, Locke. I can make my own decisions about who I spend time with."

"Why him?" I demand to know, unable to stop my mouth from running.

Being outside hasn't helped my brain to move any faster. In fact, I don't realize that she's stepped forward until she jabs a manicured nail between my pecs.

"You've been hot and cold for this whole tour, and now you're dragging me out of this very nice casino because-" She pauses and I stare down at her, thinking that there is a ring of blue around her pupil, making the pale green of her irises look almost like sea water.

Shit. I'm *drunk*. Maybe even a little more drunk than I was in Tucson with that blonde bartender.

"Because why? You don't want me to have any fun? You wanna keep me in a bubble just like my brother?"

To my horror, I see tears forming in those beautiful eyes of hers, and tequila tells me to do what I want, to follow my impulse, and I'm powerless to stop myself.

I tilt my head down slowly and cover her mouth with my own.

I wait for a long moment for her to hit me, to shove me backwards, but instead, her lips part, and she melts against me, bracing both of her palms on my chest now, moaning into my mouth, and a heat that has nothing to do with anger or tequila builds in my abdomen.

When she pulls away, I make a distressed sound in the back of my throat, chasing her lips, and she giggles, melodic and sweet.

I don't think about how I shouldn't be gazing at her the way I am. I don't think about how she's a decade younger than me, or how her brother will pound me into the ground if he finds out.

All I think about is how even though we aren't kissing anymore, my arms have somehow become looped around her waist, that hallowed space she has between her hips and the outer swell of her breasts. It seems so small, like I could almost span it with my hands. I tilt my head down again, pressing my forehead against hers.

"We could get out of here," I suggest, and surely now she'll hit me. Except, she doesn't. She takes my hand.

When I peel open my eyes the next morning, I don't remember anything after taking that double shot of Casamigos, and I'm alone in a hotel room I've never seen before.

The floors are white and gold instead of black and brown like my hotel room, and there's a big picture window. This isn't even the hotel we booked, because instead of looking out over the city lights, this one just looks out into a small alley. This was certainly not Aphrodite's Cavern.

My head pounds as I move my eyes around the room to search for clues. There aren't any, just my discarded clothes and boots on the floor. I'm in my skivvies beneath the scratchy, hotel blanket.

Something catches between my index and middle finger and I look down and see an auburn strand of hair curling around my palm. I'm struck with a memory so vivid I squeeze my eyes shut, as if someone has hit me.

All that auburn hair, curling just at the ends, spread across the white pillow, manicured nails pressing into my shoulders.

"Oh. Oh. Oh, Locke," she breathed, her head turned to the side, her bottom lip caught between her teeth.

"Look at me," I commanded, moving only my hips against her, feeling the silk of her panties brush across my cock.

Her eyes popped open, as pale and deep and sea green as the ocean.

"Motherfucker." A word I didn't use often because my mother had hated it when I was a teen, but totally merited here.

I'm in a city I know nothing about other than what I've seen in the movies, in a hotel room I don't remember checking into, with memories stitching together of the barely twenty-one-year-old little sister of my best friend arching up beneath me, moaning out my name. Not only that, but she's nowhere to be found and I can't find my phone after twenty minutes of searching.

Tequila is not and has never been my friend.

Chapter 16

Gemma

I don't get hangovers and I don't black out. Ah, the good old days. That statement, again, it's proven wrong. My head is pounding before I even attempt to peel open my eyes.

My eyelids feel sticky and I have to blink a few times to get the bleariness out of my vision. To my shock, there's a man lying beside me, the broad expanse of his back tan and wide.

The fact that I slept with a stranger is a little disconcerting, but I sit up gingerly, planning to sneak out. When I stand up, I look down at the guy snoring in the unfamiliar hotel room, curious as to what kind of guy drunk me picked out.

My hand flies to my mouth to cover it when I see Locke Kincaid's strong jaw snuggled into the pillow.

"What the fuck?" I whisper, my voice sounding muffled beneath my palm.

I rack my brain, trying to remember what happened after that last shot I took with Axel and then a memory hits me like a freight train.

His large hands tugged down my shorts, sliding back up to squeeze the flesh of my hips and I panted as he kissed along the backs of my thighs, pressing his teeth into one curve of my ass before he stood up, standing behind me. He pressed one hand down on my lower back and instantly I arched and bent over the sink, gasping as he pressed his erection against my ass.

"Want you so much, little bit," he mumbled, brushing my hair back from my shoulder and pressing his mouth there, biting gently, not quite hard enough to leave a mark.

I moaned because I wanted him to leave marks, wanted more of him, and when I opened my eyes he was staring into the mirror, giving me that smirk that was so similar to the one he'd given me in that bar bathroom, with that bartender like putty under him. I couldn't blame her, not now that I knew what it was like to have his hands all over me.

"Gemma," he moaned against me when I pressed my ass back against him.

"Say it again," I said throatily.

"Gemma," he moaned again, louder, and I turned to kiss him.

"Oh my God," I whisper, and bolt around the room, tugging on my shorts and my top, not bothering to look for my bra and underwear. I need to get out of here, and *now*. If I'm lucky, he won't remember as much as I do and it'll be like this never happened. No one but me would ever know that I lost my virginity to Locke Kincaid.

Locke makes a snuffling noise in his sleep and I turn and dart out of the room, remembering at the last minute to slip on my heels. I look around and realize that I'm doing the walk of shame in a completely unfamiliar hotel. This isn't the nice hotel attached to Aphrodite's Lounge, which I'd booked four rooms in. No, this was at best a Best Western; apparently Locke and I had the sense last night to book a different hotel so that no one would know.

If it were anyone else, I would be offended, but I didn't want my brother or any of the Spades (or anyone at all, really) to know that I hooked up with Locke, and getting a different hotel was the best way to keep it secret.

Good thing, too, because nothing like this will *ever* happen again. I won't allow myself to drink a single drop on the rest of this tour. I know the old adage about tequila making women's clothes come off, but I never knew that it was *true*.

Thankfully, I find my phone in my purse and schedule an Uber back to the casino hotel. Another memory, blurry but intense, comes floating into my mind as I ride the elevator down to the ground floor.

Locke kissed me hard, pressing me against the back railing of the elevator. His hands slid up under my shirt, skirting the outsides of my breasts and I kissed his throat and neck over and over.

"God," Locke groaned, and then he pulled away, staring down at me, his brown eyes dark with something I was too lustful and tipsy to name.

He cupped my breasts with his hands and my nipples tightened.

"Did he touch you like this?" His voice was low and husky and something about his tone shot pleasure up my spine.

"Who?" I asked, and Locke tilted his head down to kiss me, chuckling into my mouth.

"Right answer."

I shiver even though the air outside is dry and hot, rubbing my arms as I wait for the Uber. What *was* Locke talking about? Of course I hadn't advertised my virginity to the group, but all of them knew I didn't have time for a boyfriend, and they also knew how protective Jackson was.

The Uber driver doesn't even blink, and I wonder how many times he's had to pick up some girl dressed in club clothes from this hotel. This is Vegas, after all.

I manage to get into my hotel room without anyone seeing me, which is a miracle since it's nearing ten in the morning and Jackson's room is on the same floor as mine. I look in the mirror after I wash off my makeup, wondering if I look any different. I always thought it was stupid, how girls said that: "Do I look different?" As if losing your virginity was visible on the outside somehow.

I gingerly touch the marks on my throat which look red and angry. I guess in a way, it *does* show on the outside. I owe Susie Carmichael from tenth grade an apology.

Thank God I packed a sleeveless turtleneck that I can wear on our trip to the next city. Although I'm usually on top of our itinerary, after everything that happened last night, I don't even remember where we're going next or what time we're leaving. There are ten weeks left in the tour and twelve more performances, I know that, at least. Ten weeks seems like an extremely long time to ignore Locke Kincaid.

I'm grateful that I schedule most of our departures at noon or later, just because I know my boys and they aren't exactly early risers. I desperately need a shower because I smell like tequila and whatever cologne Locke uses and I look like hell, my hair is a mess.

I hope I don't have any more sudden memories about my night with Locke Kincaid, because it makes me ache in places I never have, and I'm already sore. As I step into the shower and look down at the marks on my breasts, I groan. From the brief memories I have of last night, Locke is a possessive lover, which unfortunately happens to be one of my favorite things. I guess it's because I used to read all my mother's Harlequin romance books and they were full of male leads who went crazy over any other man so much as looking at the female lead.

Since I'm inexperienced, most of my favorite things in a man are either what I've read or the guys I've been around, and unfortunately, Locke fits both of those things. He's my type, whether or not I like to admit it, at least, physically and in bed.

If I keep having flashbacks of how aggressive and possessive he is in bed, I'm going to have a hard time pretending that he doesn't exist, which is my new plan.

Between those fractured memories and the marks on my neck, breasts, and inner thighs, Locke made sure that even though I barely remember it, last night will be hard to forget.

Chapter 17

Locke

After a shower to wash the scent of Gemma Arden off me (some combination of rose and tequila which I find intoxicating), I feel a little less light-headed, even though my headache remains. I'm able to get it together long enough to find my phone, which had slid behind the headboard of the king-sized bed of this mystery hotel.

I'm stitching together clues like that stupid movie series with Bradley Cooper that Jackson made me watch half a dozen times. There's a stationary pad on the nightstand that tells me that this is a Best Western, but the street address means absolutely nothing to me. When I pull up the Uber app, I see that I searched for hotels near Aphrodite's Lounge, even though I spelled "hoetels" instead in my inebriation.

I'm grateful that I was smart enough to book a hotel a few miles away from the casino, because if I'd taken Gemma to my room, my best friend would have surely knocked my head off as soon as he found out. In fact, panic rises in my throat when I think about what might happen if Jackson finds out.

I'm not *actually* worried that he'll kill me, but he's certainly going to hit me, and he'll probably never talk to me again. He'll kick me out of the band and by all rights, he should. Although I don't exactly regret what happened with Gemma—according to my spotty memories, we both enjoyed ourselves immensely—Jackson's my best friend. He's been there for me when no one else was, and he believes in me and my music, so I feel like shit for betraying his trust. Not to mention, Gemma *hates* me. She never would have slept with me if she hadn't been drunk, and I feel like I might have taken advantage of her.

Axel doesn't seem to feel that way, though. I huff out a breath, anger flowing through me once more. Tequila made me admit that I am possessive over Gemma for reasons I can't begin to understand, and after last night? Seeing her flirt around with Axel will be ten times harder. Even if Gemma doesn't tell Jackson what happened, how am I supposed to act normal around her? Hell, I've already been acting crazy around her, especially after I found out about her fling with Axel. I'm sure that Gemma probably never wants to speak to me again, but I need to apologize, at least.

I manage to make it back to the hotel before noon when we're supposed to leave for the next city. Los Angeles, another big show. Luckily, this time it's a shorter trip, only about four hours so that I won't have to stare at Gemma for very long and have more memories of what her skin felt like beneath my palms. I keep having disjointed memories of the night before, about how she breathed out my name, and if I keep having those, it'll be difficult to even function like a remotely normal person around Gemma *or* Jackson.

By the time I make it back to the hotel, everyone is waiting for me as it's nearing two in the afternoon. No one complains, in fact even Samuel looks a little bleary-eyed and hungover. Jackson is already in the driver's seat of the tour bus, looking more put together than all the rest of us.

I pause when I climb onto the tour bus and Jackson just nods at me and I bite back a sigh of relief. Jackson's been too distracted to recognize what's been going on between us. No matter how distracted he might have been, it's clear from his appearance and demeanor that the distraction isn't because he's drinking too much again, and I'm grateful for that.

Gemma seems to be sleeping and I'm grateful for that, too, even though it makes my jaw tighten that she's sitting next to Axel, her head on his shoulder as they both doze. My face feels hot as I plop down across from them. Samuel took the back bunk as soon as he boarded the bus, face down and snoring before Jackson pulled out of the driveway.

I still can't comprehend why I feel the way I do about Gemma. Why the very idea of her panting beneath Axel the way she did with me last night makes me want to put my fist through a wall. It's not like I have *feelings* for her. I don't stick around long enough to have feelings for women... not since Janis. I've known Gemma for a long time, but I've never known her like *this*, and it's for the best that nothing like last night ever happens again.

The jealousy, part, though? That's harder to shake. I've always had a possessive streak, even with women that I've been casual with. Now that I've been with Gemma, now that I've tasted her...I just hope that the next ten weeks go by quickly.

Because if Gemma continues seeing Axel after this, instead of a wall, it might be my friend's face I put my fist through.

Chapter 18

Gemma

Hangovers suck. For once, I'm upset that the tour bus ride is only around four hours, because I don't even wake up when we stop, ending up with my head in Axel's lap when he gently shakes me awake.

"We're in LA, Gem. Time to rise and shine." As he speaks, he lets out a huge, jaw cracking yawn and I smile a little.

I can tell Axel suspects something happened between Locke and I, but I'm grateful that he doesn't ask. For as much as he'd seemed like just a flirt and a womanizer, Axel has proved himself a good friend to me. He's intuitive and can tell that I don't want to talk about last night, and I'm happy that things have turned out this way.

Locke's dead silent and won't so much as look at me, but I'm not complaining. His eyes on me would probably make me blush all over. I wince a little as I get off the tour bus after Axel, and he raises an eyebrow at me, but doesn't say a word. I had heard my girlfriends in high school talk about how sore they were after they'd lost their virginity, but I always assumed they were being dramatic.

Once again, I think that I owe my best friend Susie Carmichael from tenth grade an apology, because the ache between my legs, while not unpleasant, is certainly *there*. It's a long way from unpleasant, actually, I kind of like the way it feels, my stomach clenching with pleasure when I think about it, when I let myself remember how rough Locke had been. I find my eyes wandering as I get off the tour bus and Locke and Axel are unloading the luggage.

I see Locke's forearms bulge slightly as he tugs out one of our bigger suitcases and I bite my lip, another memory hitting me.

I closed my eyes, lost in pleasure as he moved his fingers inside me, stretching me out, one finger at first, then two, and I was making these guttural sounds in the back of my throat.

"No," Locke barked, and I felt his fingers in my hair, gentle at first and then tugging it into a ponytail, pulling so that my scalp stung. "Look at me when you come. Want you to know it's me who's making you feel this good."

My face floods with heat and Samuel gives me a look, stepping closer to me and leaning down to whisper into my ear.

"Gemma Arden, did you lose your v-card last night?"

"Oh God," I groan. "Shut up, Samuel. Not now."

"You *did!*" Samuel crows and Jackson climbs down off the bus, conveniently having waited to get off until Axel and Locke had finished unloading our luggage.

"Did what?" Jackson asks, and I look at him blankly, too dazed and hungover to be quick witted.

"She admitted that she cheated that last round of Slap-jack we played," Samuel quickly covers and I could have kissed him if I hadn't already kissed one member of the Spades.

Jackson laughs. "Only Gem could figure out a way to cheat at Slapjack."

"I'm resourceful," I quip, and Jackson ruffles my hair, which I hate, but this time I accept it without protest.

Jackson looks down at his phone.

"We made good time. Four hours until we need to leave for the concert. I'm gonna get some sleep. Wake me up if you order food, yeah?"

I nod. Jackson will *always* use petty cash to buy food and for expenses instead of his own money and lucky for him, I'd budgeted for the big appetites of the Spades. I'll order five pizzas and there won't be many leftovers.

When Jackson heads towards check in, I punch Samuel in the arm and he just laughs.

"You can tell me all about it later," he teases, and I roll my eyes. I might tell him about it, though, because it's not like I have a long list of female friends that I can call and tell.

I had plenty of them when I was in my freshman and sophomore year of high school, but when my parents were killed in a car accident one icy night, Jackson and I had to move a few hours away near our aunt and uncle and I was too devastated to try and keep in touch. Besides, we had nothing in common anymore. They were worried about boys and when they'd go off to college while I had dead parents and a brother who was working two jobs to help my aunt and uncle take care of me. I did my fair share of rebelling and sneaking out, but Jackson made sure I didn't get into any real trouble. As a result, he spent every moment he wasn't working with me, dragging me along to practices with various bands he'd had over the years, and all my friends had ended up being guys in the rock star circuit.

Not that I want to gush about Locke Kincaid, of course. But it would be nice to have someone unbiased to talk to...I may end up confiding in Samuel, after all.

For a few moments, I'm able to stop thinking about Locke and what happened last night as I head up to my room. He's gotten on the elevator before me, thankfully, because I certainly don't want to think about how he acted in the elevator last night. When I step out of the elevator, I almost bump into a man that's standing in the middle of the hall. I don't even have to look up to know that it's Locke, and I let a long breath out through my nostrils.

"Excuse me," I mumble, and Locke reaches out a hand as if to touch me, but he just hovers over my upper arm.

"C-can I talk to you?" Locke sounds uncertain, and he rarely ever sounds uncertain.

Shit.

I shrug, figuring that playing it cool is the best way to go. "I guess so."

Locke clears his throat and looks around the hallway. I look down at the itinerary I have pulled up in my phone with notes about the room numbers I'd booked and inwardly groan.

Locke and I are both on the third floor. Jackson, Samuel, and Axel all managed to get first floor rooms, those lucky bastards.

"I'm sorry about last night."

I stare at him, shocked. Of all the things I'd expected him to say, this isn't it. This is the second time Locke Kincaid has apologized to me on this tour, and I'm beginning to think he's been body snatched or something.

"You're sorry?"

Locke winces, taking my words the wrong way. I must have sounded indignant instead of just confused.

"I really am sorry. I should have never taken advantage-"

I scoff, I can't help it. As much as I'm annoyed that he remembers, the idea that he might think what happened wasn't my choice pisses me off.

"I'm not some drunk sixteen-year-old, Locke, you didn't take *advantage* of me."

Locke blinks. "I didn't?"

"*No*, you idiot. I kissed you back, didn't I?"

It's admittedly blurry, but I remember the parking lot and how he'd kissed me after I'd yelled at him. It was one of those kisses I wouldn't easily forget, even with my blood flowing with tequila.

"I guess you did," Locke says slowly, and I roll my eyes.

"You know, you're a lot of things, Locke, but I never thought you were an idiot."

Locke grins, and it lights up his whole face and my heart skips a beat.

"Little do you know."

Oh no. He's being cute. I have to get out of here immediately.

"Anyway, no harm no foul. We were drunk and angry and sometimes shit happens, right?" I babble, shifting my tote bag up on my shoulder to indicate that I'm in a hurry.

"Right," Locke responds, his smile fading. "And it can never happen again."

"Of course not!" I chirp, and that's exactly what I want, for him to agree that we can never hook up again, but it stings a little, all the same.

"Never," Locke repeats, and I huff out a breath, slightly offended.

"Yeah, never. One time thing."

Locke just nods and I take a step forward but he doesn't move, making me brush past him. Tears aren't burning at the backs of my eyes, definitely not. I don't even *like* Locke Kincaid.

It doesn't matter, anyway. We both decided. It will never happen again.

The concert in Los Angeles goes off without a hitch and we're not even halfway through the tour and I've sold over half our merchandise and records. It's a wonderful night to celebrate, but I stay away from tequila because I'm *smart*.

Instead, I go back to my old standard, filthy martinis with Ketel One, and I stick to three instead of God knows how many shots. I still have a slight headache from lack of sleep and overindulging last night, and it just gets worse when a swarm of women surrounds Locke after the show.

Jackson has once again announced that Locke wrote and produced our most popular original song, "Keyed Up," and there's a wealth of skinny Los Angeles blondes all around him. It's not that I'm jealous because he's grinning at them and accepting drinks from them. It's not that I'm jealous at *all*, but given what happened last night, it seems just a little disrespectful.

Samuel and Axel both notice the sour look on my face and Samuel looks as if he's slowly realizing something.

"Don't you dare!" I hiss, although it's more of a screech over the club music.

"You fucked Locke Kincaid," Samuel gasps, and I look around for Jackson even though I know that he couldn't possibly have heard us over the music.

Jackson is nowhere to be found, though, he's been

ducking out after every concert, but since my brother has the tendency to go off the rails if he spends too much time in bars, I'm not too concerned. In fact, I'm more relieved, since Axel is gaping at me like I'm an alien from the planet Krypton and Samuel is laughing uproariously, Jackson would definitely know something was up if he were here.

"I should have known," Axel says, and I groan and gulp down the rest of my martini.

I put my head down on the table that we're sitting at near the back of the bar.

"Everyone makes mistakes, okay?"

"I should have *known*," Axel repeats. "He glared at me like he wanted to take my head off when I made a comment..."

The guitarist trails off and I lift my head and narrow my eyes at him.

"What kind of comment, Axel?"

"Uhh..." Axel changes the subject. "It doesn't matter. The point is, Locke has had a thing for you since we were back in Tucson."

I sit up at that revelation, unable to continue giving Axel attitude about what comment he might have made.

"What? No he hasn't."

"He kinda has," Samuel agrees, and I look at him incredulously.

"What the hell are you two talking about? He's hated me forever!"

"Locke hates everybody," Axel says dryly, and Samuel nods in agreement.

"You guys are both crazy." I dismiss this whole conversation because it's making my head hurt, but at least it's taking my mind off all the blondes swarming Locke. Does he have a thing for blondes? After all, that bartender had been blonde...

"The way he acted that night in Tucson, Gem - it's obvious he was jealous," Axel insists, his words jerking me out of my thoughts.

"Jealous? Why would he be jealous?"

Axel shrugs. "He's just that kind of guy. You should have seen him with his ex, he got in a lot of bar fights over her in the early days."

"The early days?" I ask, curious. I'm beginning to understand that as much time as I've spent with the Spades, I don't know that much about their lives from before I was old enough to spend more time with them. After all, I hadn't known that Axel is divorced, and I didn't even know Locke *has* an ex-girlfriend. The only girls I'd seen around Locke had lasted two weeks, at best.

"Yeah, when they first got engaged," Axel explains, and my eyes nearly bug out of my head.

"Locke was *engaged*?"

Samuel looks unsure. "I don't know if we should be talking about this, Ax."

"Shit. I guess not." Axel looks down at his beer. "I really gotta stop drinking so much."

"It's okay," I assure him, and for a moment, everyone shuts up, lost in their own thoughts. I keep trying not to order another filthy martini because my eyes keep wandering over to Locke at the bar with all those women. It makes my stomach roll. Lots of them seem to be his own age, too.

Is that why he was so quick to say "never again?"

"Hey, Gem," Axel calls, and I look up, jerking out of my thoughts again.

"Hmm?" I ask absentmindedly, still staring over at Locke.

Axel grabs my wrist and I look up, not having noticed that he's now up.

"C'mere. I wanna prove a point."

Chapter 19

Locke

Thank God the concert went so well, and thank Los Angeles for having a wealth of attractive women who happen to be into drummers. Distraction is just what I need, and I can fight the urge to look over at Gemma as long as hot blondes are buying me drinks.

Gemma happens to look phenomenal tonight, too, going all out for our show in the city of angels. She's wearing a floor-length, sea-green dress that's slit up to her hip on both sides and clings to every curve. The color brings out her eyes and she's curled her auburn hair so that she damn near looks like a mermaid that's just gained her legs. Those damn stilettos she loves show off her calves and thighs, and the way those floral tattoos on her right thigh peeks out from that slit in her skirt makes my mouth go dry.

It had been all I could do during the concert not to stare at her dancing in the crowd. I managed to keep myself focused on the music, though, and now, I've got plenty to keep me distracted.

That is, until I hear Samuel whoop, a sound that is pretty unusual. Samuel isn't exactly a wallflower, but he doesn't exactly party, either, so I look up, a bit concerned. He looks okay, though, not too drunk, standing at the edge of the dance floor and hyping Axel up, who's dirty dancing with some girl. I laugh a little, but it fades fast when Axel spins her and I see those tiger lilies on her thigh.

I tell myself not to react, tell myself over and over that it doesn't matter, that I don't own Gemma Arden, but my caveman brain says something else and I abruptly stand up, nearly knocking a blonde off my lap.

"Hey!"

"Sorry, sweetheart," I mumble, and that's when I should have stopped. I should have taken that blonde back to the hotel and been done with the night.

I'm not very good at doing what I should, though. Goes with the territory of being a rocker, I guess.

I stalk out onto the dance floor and tap Axel on the shoulder, twice, hard.

Axel turns, giving me a surprised look so dramatic that it almost looks fake. Axel's always dramatic, though, so I don't think much of it.

"What's up?"

"I'm cutting in," I bark, and Axel grins sheepishly and steps aside.

Gemma looks up at me, her auburn hair slightly mussed, sweat beading between her breasts. She pouts at me and I want to bite that full bottom lip.

"I was having fun," she whines, but she doesn't sound drunk, not like last night.

"I'm more fun than he is," I growl, and she giggles softly and wraps her arms around my neck.

"Yeah? Guess you better prove it."

Fuck. She's cute and sassy and she looks amazing. How

am I supposed to say no to that? I'm not even much of a dancer, but now I've got to prove myself.

It's fine. I think. *It's just a dance. She said never again, right?*

* * *

An hour later, I check into a Best Western ten miles from the venue under the name James Hendrix. They only have a suite available with a kitchenette, but I would have taken a bare mattress on the floor to get my hands under that dress.

The moment we step into the room, her tugging my hand as if she can't wait, I twirl her toward me and kiss her hard, hefting her up by her ass and thighs and depositing her on the small dining room table in the suite, moving my hands to knead the flesh of her thighs. She drags her nails across my shoulders and I groan.

"Kiss me," she pouts, pointing at her lips cutely, and I grin up at her as I kneel on the floor.

"Oh, I will, little bit. Just not there."

I slide my hands under her thick thighs, pulling her to the edge of the table. She cries out and it's an almost guttural sound that makes my jeans feel even tighter. I'm glad that I didn't drink much back at the bar, glad that I will remember this scene vividly tomorrow morning, because Gemma's body is fucking *perfect,* and I tell her as much.

"Shut up and-" she doesn't finish because I press my mouth against her sex and she gasps out my name, and that's a sound I'll replay over the coming weeks. She tastes like sweet musk and all my filthiest dreams.

I moan against her and she clenches her thighs around my head as I knead her ass with my hands, supple beneath my palms. If I had been told to mold a woman with my perfect body type, it would be Gemma, with her thick thighs and firm ass with just a slight jiggle, her slim waist and small, pert breasts.

I slide a finger inside her, and then two, as my lips wrap around her bud. She clenches around them, making my cock ache. I remember how tight and slick she'd felt around me, that is the one vivid memory that I have of the other night. She cries out my name when she comes and I can't wait any longer.

When we'd ended up kissing in the alley outside the venue, I'd told myself that I'd take my time with Gemma tonight, since it was likely that we'd never do this again.

That doesn't happen, though, because she's so gorgeous and she tastes so good; I can't wait to have her, standing up. Gemma whines when my fingers slide out of her.

"Be patient, little bit," I murmur, but I'm not patient at all, fumbling with my belt and whipping it off to toss it on the floor.

Gemma's green eyes are hungry on my face, her pouty bottom lip caught between her teeth.

"Locke," she breathes, and I love the way she does that, how she says my name like she can barely bear to speak but just *has* to say it.

"Say it again," I command, not bothering to take off my clothes or hers, just pulling my cock free from my jeans and boxer briefs and sliding myself against her slick heat, but not inside her. Not yet.

Gemma writhes on the table and I smirk down at her pouty expression. Her cheeks redden as I watch her work her hips against me, but she keeps her mouth closed.

"Should have known you won't do what's asked of you, little bit. Always pegged you as a brat."

I slide myself against her, working my tip against her bud and she groans throatily.

"Say it," I command again. "Say my name."

Gemma huffs out a breath and then looks me right in the eye and sticks her tongue out at me, not lewdly but like a brat who didn't get her way, and it surprises a laugh out of me.

"All right," I say, amicably enough. "Guess I'll have to make you."

I lean over, nearly doubling myself to suck on the tongue she'd stuck out at me. She moans into my mouth, clawing her fingernails down my back. It stings through my thin t-shirt and I hiss and my hips jut forward, sliding into her after one failed try where I just slide up her slick lips again.

Gemma bites my bottom lip, the little minx, but that stings just as sweet as her nails on my back. I rock into her slowly, gritting my teeth as she pulls away from my mouth to gasp in a breath. I'm holding back, and not because I think I'll hurt her. I'm no slouch in the size department but I'm not huge, either, and Gemma's all but begging me to go rougher and harder.

That's why I can't go rougher and harder, because she wants me to and I want her to say it. I've got this burning need for her to say my name, acknowledge that it's me she wants sliding her across this kitchen table.

Gemma has turned her face away, though, so I lean up and use one of my hands to rip down the plunging neckline of her dress, exposing her breasts. I hear the seam pop, but I don't care, just cup her right breast in my left hand (a perfect handful), squeezing gently before pinching her nipple between my middle finger and thumb.

"Ah!" she cries out, her green eyes shooting to mine, her hips bucking up toward my thrusts.

"You know you want to say it," I croon, smirking, and Gemma glares up at me for only a second before her eyes go unfocused as I roll her nipple between my fingers, more gently this time.

Her mouth opens in a silent moan and she grinds her hips up in a move that has me gasping.

"Please," she begs, finally, and I think about denying her again but she licks her lips, focuses on my face. "*Locke.*"

That's it, folks, I can't hold back anymore, already close to bursting from all the foreplay and the way she'd tasted on my tongue. I snap my hips into her, panting, angling up because of the direction she's grinding against me.

I'm not a super expert in the bedroom, but I know my way around and I pay attention.

Before the Spades, I'd been with Janis, so relationship sex is what I'm used to. I don't do a lot of one-night stands. Usually they turn into flings, at least, simply because I'm not the charmer that Axel or Jackson are, and because, in my opinion, one-night stands simply aren't very fun. I can't know a woman's triggers to orgasm in one night (unless it's some rare marathon session), can't bring them pleasure in the same way that I can if we've hooked up multiple times.

So when I *do* have a one (or in this case two) night stand, I'm extra observant, intuitive even. I watch what she does, how she moves, and from there I can discern where she wants me to touch her, how she wants me to move my hips.

I once said something to the guys about why I preferred flings to one-night stands, and Axel told me that was a weirdly logical and scientific way to look at sex. Maybe that's true, but I can't help feeling pride that Gemma is

115

begging for *me* instead of him right now, despite how this tour had started.

Besides, if I start thinking about sex with my emotions... I know where that leads, and I'm not about to go through that again.

I focus on Gemma again and try every trick I know to last, but the way her mouth is open, face contorted, I know she's close and it's only a few moments before she calls out my name again, louder, and I spill inside her.

"Never again," Gemma announces as she's tucking those perfect breasts of hers back into her dress and then they fall right back out because the seam is ripped.

I manage to stifle a laugh and I tug off my t-shirt and put it over her head as she sputters.

She glares at me after she puts her arms through the sleeves.

God, she's cute. I blink, not liking where that thought might lead and focus instead on how I can see her nipples through my shirt.

My tongue darts out to wet my lips. Something about a woman wearing my clothes has always done something for me. It's not Gemma specifically. It's *not*.

"Never again," I agree, and raise an eyebrow. "After tonight."

Gemma purses her lips as if thinking. "I mean, we didn't even use the bed that we paid for."

"That *I* paid for," I remark and she narrows her eyes.

"You're talking yourself right out of-"

I cut her off by grabbing her around the waist and throwing her over my shoulder, depositing her on the bed while she lets out a giggle that makes my chest expand.

Chapter 20

Gemma

ever again. Never again. It becomes a mantra in my head. I tell it to myself before every show. It's not exactly as if I can avoid Locke during the tour. We're all in close quarters on the bus and at the hotel I end up running into him at meals, no matter how much I try to stick closer to Axel or Samuel.

I'm avoiding Jackson, too, mostly because as my big brother, he can always tell when I have a secret. He always knows when I'm lying, and I'm more than grateful that he's been scarce ever since Albuquerque. I know I should be worried, but this isn't like before, when Jackson went off the rails a bit after his last breakup. He's being secretive, but he's also showing up on time for shows, barely drinking after, and he seems...happy. Happy in a way I haven't seen him in a long time. Maybe since before our parents died.

Since I have my own secret—which will *never happen again*—I can't really judge, can I? So I let Jackson sneak around and I cover for him around Samuel and Axel. Locke doesn't ask questions, but then again, I guess he's distracted too.

I bend over further than I need to in order to pick up my tote bag from where I'd put it on the ground while checking us into the hotel in Oklahoma City. I smirk when I glance over my shoulder and Locke is staring.

Maybe I've been making a point to wear yoga shorts and tight jeans ever since Locke made a pillow-talk comment about my "perfect body," but who could blame me? For a girl who's as inexperienced as I am, having a man who looks like Locke appreciating my form is flattering, to say the least. If I'm honest with myself, it's more than flattering. It's downright intoxicating. Locke Kincaid is more intoxicating than the tequila shots I take with Axel or the filthy martinis that I order for myself.

Oklahoma City is our eighth show and our seventh week on the road, and I'm beginning to forget what my apartment looks like. More than that, I hadn't even *used* the hotel rooms I booked for myself in Denver or Olympia. I spent the nights after those shows in a hotel room that Locke paid for, last minute. It's like we're repeating that night in Vegas over and over, except not.

In Denver, Locke and I had an argument about the set list. The rest of the Spades stared at us as we yelled at each other, mostly because I never messed with the set list. I wanted the show to open with "Keyed Up" because I thought it would draw in more people from outside, but Locke was determined for it to be the last song, like at all the rest of the concerts. I was so mad about it I was turning red, and finally, Jackson decided things by siding with Locke and I stormed off with Axel to drown out my anger with a couple of tequila shots.

After the show, Locke cornered me near the bathrooms in a full circle to when I'd caught him with that blond bartender.

"You here to apologize?" I asked, crossing my arms.

Locke raised an eyebrow but I could see the ghost of a smile at the corner of his mouth, that dimple popping out just slightly.

"I was going to ask the same to you."

I opened my mouth to curse at him but Locke glanced over his shoulder and then back at me before he grabbed the back of my head, leaning down to kiss me hard and fast before pulling away.

We snuck out the back, and before I knew it, Locke picked me up, grinding against me against the back of the tour bus. He nipped the base of my throat and I moaned, shocked when he clapped his hand over my mouth.

I should have been furious with him for the argument and the way he was trying to order me around, but my body was on fire. I ground my hips against him desperately and he squeezed my hip bone to stop me.

"Shh," he whispered into my ear and then I heard Axel babbling to Jackson, something about IHOP vs. Waffle House, and I froze, my eyes popping open to look at Locke.

He slowly lowered me to the ground and took a step back from me, placing his finger against his lips with a slow smirk.

God, I hated him so much.

An hour later, we were back at the hotel and I was determined to go straight to my room and take a hot shower.

Locke was on the third floor and I was on the sixth, so it shouldn't have been too hard to stay away. My brother said good night in the lobby since he was on the first floor, and I gave him a thin smile.

When Samuel and Axel got off on the second floor, Locke didn't say a word to me, but when the elevator doors opened, he wrapped his fingers around my wrist and tugged me out into the hallway.

I could have protested, but I didn't, and instead, I woke up at six in the morning with my head on his bare chest.

I told myself I wouldn't do that in Olympia, but guess where I woke up?

* * *

But none of that matters because *never again*. Yes, it's fun, hooking up with Locke, and maybe it's even more fun because it's forbidden, because my brother will lose his mind if he finds out, maybe it's even more fun because Locke is older, more experienced. I might have been a virgin before this tour, but I was no blushing school girl. I'd made out with guys before, even let a couple of them get to third base, and I always assumed that going all the way would just be a step above that.

Turns out, instead of a step, it's more like a whole damn staircase. Before Locke, I always figured I could please myself better than any man could, but *now?* It's like I never knew what I was missing and now that I've had it, I crave it. I crave *him*. I crave his mouth and his body and the way that he looks at me, something almost predatory in his brown eyes.

I'm just going to have to make do with the sideways glances he gives me, though, because I *cannot* allow myself to get in any deeper with Locke Kincaid. The sex is amazing and it's fun to sneak around, but at the end of the day, I know that it can't go anywhere. I've known Locke since I was nineteen, and he's never had a steady girlfriend.

At the beginning of the tour, I focused on Axel because I knew that it'd be casual for both of us. I like Axel well enough for us to part as friends, and he's relatively harmless even if he's a bit of a womanizer. Jackson is close with all the members of the Spades, but he's not *particularly* close with Axel, so even if he found out, it wouldn't be catastrophic.

Locke, on the other hand, is exactly my type and we've never been friends. If I end up catching feelings for him, I'll never forgive myself. There's also the fact that Locke is Jackson's best friend, and he's always trusted him to keep an eye on me at venues when Jackson couldn't be there. If he finds out that it was Locke Kincaid who was the danger all along... let's just say catastrophic isn't a strong enough word.

Right now, everything is fine. I don't like Locke, and if we stop now, I can keep myself from falling into a cycle of continuing to hook up with him. My friend Susie always told me there was a science to falling in love and it was about the amount of time you spent alone with someone. According to Susie, in order to keep a fling casual, you can't spend more than a few hours with them when you hook up, and you can't spend a total of more than two weeks alone with them. Luckily for me, spending that much time with Locke isn't even a possibility, even with Jackson distracted.

I sure miss Susie now that I finally have something going on with my sex life. I always felt left out during girl talk since I spent so much time at dive bars and mosh pits. I met a lot of guys, had a lot of drinks bought for me, but I never had much to say when Susie and the couple other girls I spend time with talked about men. Now, I'm bursting at the seams to talk to someone, but Samuel and Axel are absolutely not interested in hearing about my sex life, and besides, they're his *friends*. It's not like I can be honest and gush about how great sex with Locke is to them.

God, maybe it's for the best that I don't have anyone to talk to about this. Even my own thoughts sound like a teenage girl and it makes me cringe.

My mind is racing in the elevator and I don't even

notice that Locke has moved to the back and is standing behind me until he leans forward and murmurs in my ear.

"I think you're starting to like me, little bit."

I jump as his hand slowly moves to my lower back.

I scoff. "Don't get your hopes up.

Locke chuckles and I can feel his breath on my bare shoulder. I shiver and he moves his hand lower, squeezing the curve of my right ass cheek just hard enough that I let out a squeak.

Jackson, at the front of the elevator, turns to look at me, raising a dark blond eyebrow.

I cover it with a cough. "Think I'm coming down with something."

"Maybe you shouldn't come tonight, Gem," my brother offers, looking concerned, and instead of arguing like I usually would, I nod. I can guarantee that I won't end up hooking up with Locke if I stay at the hotel.

"I can handle the merchandise," Locke offers, and I look up at him, surprised. Locke is the least sociable of all the Spades, and he never offers that kind of help.

Jackson laughs. "Yeah, all the ladies seem to love you after I announced that you wrote our title song."

I stiffen and something tightens in my throat. I remember that night in Los Angeles, when all those blondes converged around Locke and it felt like I was the last picked in high school volleyball all over again.

I tune out whatever the guys are saying until my brother says my name once and then twice.

"Gem? You really are sick."

"I-" I shake my head. "Yeah, I guess I should go lie down."

Jackson's brow furrows as the elevator doors ding open. The only hotel I could find close enough to the venue downtown had twenty-two floors, and Jackson was on eleven.

"Locke, walk her to her room, will you?"

Locke nods, but I shake my head frantically.

"N-no, Axel can do it." Axel is my best friend and I trust myself not to kiss him. I can't say the same about Locke.

Jackson gives me a strange look. "Axel is on the same floor as me, Locke is on the one above yours."

I feel nauseous, and I wonder if what my mother said was true. She'd always said that if you told a lie big enough, it would become true, and sure enough, I'm beginning to feel sick.

"Don't worry," Locke assures Jackson, and I feel dizzy. I have no idea how Locke manages to act so nonchalant when the simple act of him walking me to my room makes me feel like I'm going to vomit.

Jackson nods to him. "Besides, you know all the technical stuff is like Greek to me. Fill Locke in."

I don't even try to nod again, worrying that it will make the sudden wave of vertigo worse, and Jackson frowns at me when he gets off the elevator, wheeling his overnight bag behind him.

"Get some rest," he commands, and I give him a thumbs up instead of risking the nod. Instead of asking questions, he just shakes his head quizzically and heads toward his room.

Axel, on the other hand, stays on the elevator for a long moment, looking between me and Locke.

"You want me to walk you, sweetheart?" he asks, and I smile at him gratefully. Axel's just looking out for me, he knows that Locke and I hooked up in Vegas but I haven't mentioned anything else. I'm glad that we've become closer friends on the tour, and I make a mental note to check in with him about how things are going with his ex.

"Nope," Locke says firmly before I can speak. "We're good."

I look up at him and he's just staring at Axel, his face blank, jaw locked.

Why does he look so good when he looks so serious? Not that he doesn't have a great smile—that dimple makes him look positively rakish when he grins, but something about how tight and square his jaw looks like this, the long line of his nose...

I *must* be sick. My mother was right.

Axel touches my shoulder gently before getting off the elevator.

Locke draws in a long breath through his nostrils.

The doors close and I look at the numbers going up with acid rising in my throat. We're on the 18th floor and I really don't know if I'll make it before losing my breakfast. The link sausages I ate at Waffle House desperately want out.

Twelve... up it goes... thirteen...I focus on the numbers and try to breathe in through my nose...fourteen...out through my mouth...fifteen...the elevator lurches to a stop at sixteen and I nearly tumble over, leaning on to Locke for balance.

"Hey, now," Locke murmurs, gentle and low and almost soothing as he rights me, keeping an arm around my shoulder. "Are you really sick, little bit?"

I make a noncommittal noise in the back of my throat, unable to look at anything but the red light of the elevator floor number.

An older woman, around sixty, shuffles on to the elevator and she looks at the elevator arrow and then back at us sheepishly.

"I'm so sorry, I thought this was going down to the lobby."

"No worries," I choke out, and everything would have been fine if Locke didn't squeeze my shoulder. I lean in to him, his touch making me feel less queasy.

The woman looks at Locke and then back to me.

"How long have you two been married?"

My face goes pale and I look up at Locke but he's straight faced.

"Newlyweds," he deadpans, and I choke back laughter.

The woman gets back off the elevator and I want to hit him but I don't think I have the balance, so instead I allow myself to laugh.

Locke laughs with me, and for a moment, my heart skips a beat. I don't read into it. I'm sick, after all.

"Should have booked us the honeymoon suite," I crack, and Locke laughs, too, but low instead of loud and open like usual when I happen to make the right joke.

Locke has this deadpan wit that used to confuse me, but lately, I've been catching on and he's quite funny, really. He's not out there like Axel and Jackson or understated and witty like Samuel, but his sense of humor appeals to me.

Locke insists on carrying my luggage and I let him, mostly because I'm having to hold on to the wall for balance. He deposits everything inside and I gingerly lie face down on the bed. I close my eyes and expect to hear the click of the door behind him any second.

Instead, I hear the bathroom door open and the running of water, and then a cool cloth on the back of my neck.

I let out a long sigh. So good, I was almost sweating although my skin felt cool to the touch, a clear sign that I am indeed coming down with something.

"I'm never lying again," I say, and it comes out in a slur.

I'm more tired than I thought I was, but this tour has had us all running ragged.

"Good to know," Locke murmurs agreeably even though I'm not making any sense, and he rubs the middle of my back.

Jackson used to do that when I was little and couldn't sleep. I hadn't wanted to give up my crib so when my dad finally got rid of it I'd climb out of my little twin bed and crawl into Jackson's bed, which was a full size. He was barely a teenager and he'd grumble for me to go to our parents' room but I never did, just whined until he'd rub my back and put me to sleep.

If this was Jackson or even Samuel or Axel rubbing my back, it might feel just as comforting, and I tell myself that's what this is. As I start to drift off, though, I wish that Locke would climb into bed with me and hold me, remembering how his closeness had nearly taken away my nausea in the elevator.

I don't realize I've said it out loud until the covers shift and a pair of strong, warm arms go around my waist, pulling me close, my back against his chest. I think I'm delirious because I hear my voice, but I'm not sure what I'm saying or where I am anymore, and Locke simply spreads his hands across my belly and the pressure and warmth of them make my stomach hurt less, and the queasiness less awful.

I'm lying diagonally across the bed, near the waste-basket just in case, but Locke doesn't complain about the lack of space for his big frame. He hums softly into my ear, some melody I've never heard.

"Did you write that?" I slur, half asleep, and he nods, his chin pressing into my shoulder. "When? I've never heard it."

"Just now."

"Can it be my song?"

Locke is quiet for a long moment and I'm drifting off to sleep despite how bad I feel, so later, I'm not sure if I dreamed his answer.

"I think it already is."

* * *

I wake to my alarm going off, one I'd neglected to turn off after I decided not to go to the concert. It's cold in my room and I'm still feeling too sick to question why I'm disappointed that I'm alone.

I get up and wash my face and send a barrage of texts to Locke to make sure he remembers each detail of the show. Infuriatingly, he only sends back a thumbs up emoji, but honestly, I know that he knows what to do. Locke has been in the music business since I was still jailbait, and Jackson was right. My brother's not so good at the financial part of music. Locke can handle it, and I'm not too worried as I settle back into bed, nibbling on saltine crackers I found in my purse. I'm angry with myself for eating pork since it doesn't always agree with me, but this seems like overkill. I feel pale and clammy and everything aches.

It's a strange feeling, not quite like when I had food poisoning in high school from some gas station sushi, but close enough. Something feels off, unstable in a way, and it leads me to text Axel, who was the only other one of us who ordered the link sausages. I text that I'm sick and ask if the sausages are disagreeing with him, too. He quickly texts back that he's healthy as a horse and I frown down at my phone but shrug, turning on the television.

An hour later, Axel sends me the weirdest text I've ever gotten from a man in my life.

Gemma, is your period late?

I nearly choke on my saltine crackers and I'm about to ask what the fuck he's talking about when it slowly dawns on me. I've taken birth control religiously since I was thirteen because of awful period cramps that kept me out of gym class, and on some months, out of school for two days. I haven't been sexually active until this tour, so maybe I've skipped a day here and there, but surely....

It's been so busy that I haven't been great about keeping track, so I frantically open my tracker app to see the little liquid drop of red and have to scroll back over a month to see it.

Two weeks. I'm nearly two weeks late.

I don't respond to Axel, and eventually, he texts me again while I'm staring blankly at the television, which has some kind of QVC channel playing, but I can't be bothered to pick up my phone.

Two weeks late.

What the hell am I going to do now?

Chapter 21

Locke

I 'm not the clingy type, even in a long-term relationship instead of a casual fling, so I tell myself there's no reason to get bent out of shape about Gemma avoiding me over the next few days. She's sick, after all, and just because she's stuck right next to Axel at all times shouldn't give me a reason to worry. But I'm possessive over even casual partners, so I can't help sitting between them on the tour bus from Oklahoma City to Dallas.

Gemma looks pale and I'm a little worried about her.

"Do you want me to get you a ginger ale?" I ask her softly when we stop at a gas station, and she favors me with a weak smile.

"Thanks, Axel's grabbing one for me."

Of course he is, I think, and then my mouth runs away with me.

"If you were...you know...with someone else, you'd tell me, wouldn't you?"

I hate myself the second I say it because her green eyes flash with anger.

"And why would I do that?" she snaps and gets up to storm off the bus into the gas station.

I'm alone on the bus, so I groan and sit back in the seat. Gemma's comment doesn't make me feel better in the slightest.

What does that mean, anyway? If she's still sleeping with Axel...I can't even think about it without red rage forming in the corners of my vision. I press the heels of my hands into my eyes until I see spots and when I remove them, Samuel is staring at me with a raised eyebrow.

"You gonna do anything about that?" he asks, as if this is a hole in one of my drums or something.

"About what?" I ask, playing dumb. I can see Jackson milling around the front of the gas station, on the phone with someone, probably a girl. Probably *the* girl, from what I can tell by his furrowed brow. Jackson hasn't picked up a single girl in weeks, as far as I know, so someone must have hooked him. Unlike myself and Axel, Jackson falls into relationships sometimes after a fling.

"About *Gemma*," Samuel replies, sounding exasperated, as if he thinks I'm an idiot. He probably does.

Hell, *I* think I'm an idiot, and not for what I just said to Gemma or my jealousy. I'm an idiot for feeling the way I do about her. I worry about her all the time, and that started happening even before she got sick. I'm worried about what she's doing when she's alone with Axel, worried about someone bumping her around during a concert, worried someone will follow her to a club bathroom and harass her. Most of all, I'm an idiot for worrying if she likes me as much as I've come to like her.

I'm an idiot because I *do* like her. I buy Zero bars and blue Takis at every gas station we go to. I've got a whole damn tote bag full of the things, just because they're her favorite snacks. I told myself when I started that I was just making myself a backup for one of our long stretch trips, but so far, I haven't eaten a single one, passing a bag of Takis to her on the tour bus or handing her a Zero bar after the show. She doesn't always eat before the shows, and of course, I worry about that, too.

That's the thing. I get possessive over women that I barely know, so that doesn't tip me off, it's all the *worrying* that means that I like her. I only worry at that level about the people I care most about. So now I'm stuck in a casual fling relationship with my best friend's little sister and she doesn't seem to like me any more than she did when we first met—at least, not outside the bedroom. And now, my possessive nature isn't just possessive, but *jealous*, and that's a much harder emotion for me to control.

It's not like I don't have good reason to be jealous, given how she's running around with our lead guitarist. Not just that, but given the way things went the last time I liked a girl...let's just say I have plenty of baggage.

"Nothing," I say flatly.

"Every woman isn't Janis, Locke." Samuel says softly, as if he read my mind, and I flinch.

"Of course not," I reply, grinning, and look over to make sure Jackson is still out of earshot. "Gemma's much hotter than Janis ever was."

"Can't wait to watch Jack beat your ass," Samuel mutters under his breath, and I can't help but smile.

Samuel's ticked off at me, but he won't rat me out. I reach over and ruffle his hair and he groans.

Axel jumps up into the tour bus looking like he hasn't slept in a week, but I guess we all kind of look like that. I definitely shouldn't assume that he's been up all night with Gemma.

She's been too sick for that, I tell myself. My gut still feels like it's in knots thinking about Axel comforting her and bringing her ginger ale when she's not feeling well, though. That's not exactly *worse* than my imagination, but it's not better, either.

I want that to be *my* job, and therein lies the problem. I like Gemma, and that's a problem, but if I fall in *love*... When that happens, I risk everything.

I fell for Janis Childs when I was twenty years old, and it was a flame that burned until I was nearly thirty, off and on.

We moved in together when we were twenty-two, after a few splits here and there and got engaged when we were twenty-four. One year in, she told me that she was over-whelmed at work and that my music was going nowhere. It hurt, but she was right, and I wanted to take care of her. It became more important than anything else to me.

I quit the band I was in and started working construction full-time to make her happy. On my twenty-seventh birthday, I attended a concert for Dirty Liars, the band I had been a drummer for with a few of my friends.

The band name turned out to be a warning.

I caught Janis with the lead singer and a close friend of mine, Mike. They were making out in an alley behind the club and I couldn't even muster the anger to hit him, just stared at her as she babbled.

"Locke. I was going to tell you-"

I walked away, not saying a word as she chased me down the street. I didn't say a word when I packed my things, either, or even when she threw a ceramic frog at my head. I ducked and it crashed against the wall and I moved into a hotel room and was drunk for a solid week.

I was a mess until I met Jackson and began playing with

the Spades. Getting back into music brought me back, and I was grateful for it.

Gemma climbs back on to the bus slowly, holding on to the rails, and I immediately stand up at the same time that Axel steadies her.

I sit back down, gritting my teeth so hard that my jaw aches, and Gemma won't so much as look at me.

This is going to be the longest road trip in the world.

Chapter 22

Gemma

I hate Locke Kincaid. I hate blue Takis because I love them but now they make me want to puke, I hate this tour bus, I hate the heat in the Midwest, and I *hate* Locke Kincaid for doing this to me.

I glare at him and Locke gives me a smile, that half one that shows the dimple in his right cheek and I narrow my eyes. That's *exactly* what got me into this mess, that smile. It's the same one he had given me that first night that he'd hooked up with that bartender and made me question everything.

I huff out a breath and turn back to the cards I've got lined up along the floor, but I can't find a jack of spades no matter what I do so I throw the cards and they scatter across the floor. Samuel raises an eyebrow at me but no one says a word. Everything and everyone seems to irritate me these days, I even snap at Samuel when he offers to help me off of the tour bus when we arrive at the hotel in Dallas.

"You need me to walk you to your room again, little bit?" Locke asks me on the elevator, leaning down so only I can hear him, and I shake my head furiously.

"Absolutely not."

Locke sighs, which is a little dramatic in my opinion, and I take in a deep breath so that I don't snap at him.

He's watching Axel like a hawk, which normally, would just make me laugh and tease him. In fact, I kind of like it when Locke goes all protective and possessive, and it's certainly made the sex interesting, but right now, all I need is a damn pregnancy test. Axel's the only person in the world who knows, and it's not like I can sneak out with a tour bus full of the band's equipment in the middle of the night with both Jackson and Locke watching out for me since I've been sick.

I'm googling "will Postmates deliver a pregnancy test" as I'm walking down the hallway when Samuel gasps behind my shoulder. He's been following me since he's on the same floor as me, and apparently, my brother and Locke Kincaid think I can't walk a hundred feet without supervision.

"You're *pregnant?*"

"Stop reading over my shoulder!" I bark.

"I'm sorry," Samuel apologizes, wide eyed and holding his hands up as if in surrender and I open my mouth and everything just spills out.

"I don't *know* if I'm pregnant because my brother watches me like I'm a wayward toddler and the only person who knows is Axel and Locke is watching him as if he's on an America's Most Wanted list and I'm *sick* all the time and I don't know what to do!" I burst out, tears rolling down my face.

"Aw, Gem."

Samuel pulls me into his arms and I sob against his chest for a moment.

"Take a deep breath. There's a Walgreen's right around

the corner, I'll grab one for you. I want some Oreos anyway."

I sniffle, looking up at him. "Will you get me the vanilla Oreos?"

"I thought you hated the vanilla Oreos?" Samuel looks confused.

"I *do,* but now that's all I want to eat!" I wail.

Samuel wants to laugh, I can tell, but he holds back and I'm grateful because I cannot seem to stop my eyes from leaking.

It doesn't mean you're pregnant, I think to myself as Samuel promises to hurry back with the test (and the vanilla Oreos). *It just means you aren't sleeping.*

That much is true, I'm not sleeping much at all between hooking up with Locke and our punishing road trip and concert schedule. Everyone gets irritable on long trips and with little sleep. It'll be fine. Right? Besides, it's not like I'm hooking up with Locke anymore, is it? Since I'm doing all I can to stay as far away from him as possible ever since I realized I was late.

* * *

Samuel returns with a Walgreen's bag full of blue Powerade, vanilla Oreos, and three brands of pregnancy tests and I could kiss him if my mouth didn't taste like nervous vomit. Then again, Locke Kincaid kissing me is what got me into this mess so I'm not surprised. I text Axel that I got a test and before I even make it to the bathroom, there's a knock on my hotel door.

As soon as I open the door, Axel sneaks inside like we're doing a drug deal.

"You got the stuff?" he asks, and I choke back a barrage of nearly hysterical laughter.

I shake the bag. "There's three, so I'm chugging Powerade."

Axel looks in the bag. "That's the good one, I think."

I raise an eyebrow at him. "How would you know?"

Axel shrugs. "I've got a sister and plenty of girls I know have had scares, okay?"

"Girls you *know*, huh?" I snicker. "In the biblical way, I take it."

Axel grins and I roll my eyes as he hands me the test.

The box is pink and white and the instructions are simple enough—pee on the stick and in five minutes it will have two lines if you're pregnant and one line if you're not.

"So, I'm praying for one line," I mutter, and Axel nods.

"Unless..." he starts, and I shake my head.

"No way. I'm not pregnant, this is gonna be fine. I just caught a bug because I haven't been sleeping well."

"Okay," Axel says, as if he thinks I'm crazy, and before my blood starts to boil I go to the bathroom and take the test, sitting the capped test on the back of the toilet before exiting the room.

As I exit, a sense of calm comes over me. Women have pregnancy scares all the time, right? Susie, my best friend from high school, had a few when we were young, even, but everything turned out okay.

Axel juggles his leg anxiously and I want to push him off the end of my bed, but I don't. He seems almost as anxious as I am, as if this is his problem too, and while I appreciate the support, I find it strange. I mean, I know he's kind of a womanizer, or was before this whole situation with his ex-wife, but how many scares could he possibly have had with girls he was only with a few nights? I wonder if he's ever had a scare with his ex-wife, but every time I mention that situation, Axel gets all mopey, so I keep my mouth shut.

I jump when the timer goes off on my phone and walk calmly to the bathroom. Picking up the test, I clearly detect one line in the test area, so the test isn't faulty, good. And one *very* faint blue line in the results area. I don't make a sound, just start to shake the test and Axel grabs my arm, knowing by my blank face what the results are.

"It's not an Etch-a-Sketch, Gem," he cracks, and I laugh a little hysterically before I burst into tears.

After I calm down (relatively, since my life is coming apart at the seams), Axel sits me down on the edge of the bed.

"What are you going to do?"

I worry my bottom lip between my teeth. "I don't...I don't know."

"I mean, are you going to..." Axel trails off as if he doesn't want to say it, and in fact, I'm not sure I've made that decision yet until I find myself nodding.

"Yeah, yeah. I'm gonna keep her. I just don't know if I'm going to tell him."

"It's...it's Locke's, right?" Axel asks hesitantly, and this time, I *do* push him off the bed.

"Of course, it is!" I snap, and then help him off the floor in a half-assed apology. "You won't say anything, will you?"

Axel looks offended. "Of course not."

I wipe at my wet face. My eyes and cheeks feel puffy and I lean my head against Axel's chest. "Thank you for being my friend."

Axel rubs soothing circles on my back and I take in a deep, shaky breath, pulling away and plopping down on the bed.

"Now get out of my room so I can contemplate all my many, many mistakes."

Axel chuckles, heading to the door, and I sit up.

"Wait!" He looks back, concerned.

"Give me the bag with the vanilla Oreos in it."

Chapter 23

Locke

Gemma's acting weird, and not normally weird. Normally weird would be ignoring me or being sassy toward me, but now she's outright *mean* to me, and that's unusual. Because of her illness, I pass it off as her being irritable, but the thing is, she's not irritable with Axel, and that's what pisses me off.

It's like Gemma and Axel are attached at the hip, and Samuel sometimes seems in on it, too. Jackson doesn't seem to care, but then again, lately he doesn't seem to care about anything but the shows we do and sneaking around after. I don't think he's slept a single night in the hotels we booked in four shows now, and I'm not asking questions because I don't want him to suspect me of something.

Not that I'm doing anything nefarious right now, anyway—Gemma won't even look at me except to tell me I'm an idiot, even when I try to give her a Zero bar or a bottle of Powerade. She seems to have one around all the time, along with vanilla Oreos, which I've always loved and she says she hates.

If I still felt the way I did when we started things,

Gemma ignoring me would be a godsend. It would get her out of my hair and keep me from having to break things off. Unfortunately, I've allowed myself to develop feelings for a twenty-one-year-old girl, and I'm chasing her around trying to tell her how I feel.

I know that I haven't been the most open to relationships in the past, and I know what Gemma thinks of me, but the only way to change the way she thinks is to *talk* to her, no matter how worried I am about what might happen in the future.

God knows I don't want to end up in the same place I was after I left Janis.

Gemma's different, I tell myself. *She's not like Janis.*

It's hard to convince myself of that, though, when she's glaring daggers at me and smiling at Axel when he brings her a drink after the show in Atlanta, something light colored. She downs about three of them and I'm a little concerned about how much she's drinking. There it goes again, that concern that I have when I care about someone. It should be terrifying but right now, all I want to do is talk to Gemma.

I mill around the concert hall which has a full bar, but I'm not drinking and barely speaking to anyone. I'm seething because Gemma ignores my very existence but keeps talking to Axel in hushed whispers, their heads close together. Jealousy and worry are a bad combination, and my stomach feels sick.

"Can I talk to you, little bit?" I ask her when Axel finally goes to the bathroom.

"Don't call me that," she snaps, and that's when *I* snap, wrapping my fingers around her wrist and tugging her up.

She's surprised and bounces against my chest but she doesn't fight me, just like before. I lead her outside and she's breathing a bit hard but I don't have it in me to ask her how she's feeling at the moment, after she's been drinking and chatting with our guitarist for hours.

"I *need* to talk to you, Gemma," I say firmly, and she looks up at me, seeming a little pale. "I want to...I *need* to tell you something." I'm angry and frustrated, but suddenly, I feel shy and hesitant. What if she really *is* still sleeping with Axel? What if she's chosen him instead of me? What if I tell her I like her and she gives me the "let's just be friends" speech?

"It's not the right time, Locke," Gemma says, her words slow, and I wonder if the alcohol is hitting her.

"You shouldn't have let Axel buy you all those drinks," I scold, without even meaning to, and Gemma frowns.

"He didn't-"

"And what's going on with you and Axel, anyway? I asked if you were seeing someone else and you wouldn't tell me, and now-"

"Locke-" Gemma puts a hand over her mouth but I keep going.

"I just wanted to tell you that I...I don't feel the same way that I used to about this, and I think we need to define things because I'm going kind of nuts, little bit. I *like* you, in a way that means that it makes me crazy to think about you and Axel..." I trail off because somewhere in the middle of my tirade, Gemma runs off into the back, throwing up in the bushes outside of the venue.

Before I can go and comfort her, I realize that Gemma has dropped her phone on the pavement and I pick it up. I'm examining it for cracks when a text notification pops up from Axel on her locked screen.

Where did you go? I thought we were going to talk about the baby tonight.

I furrow my brow, confused, and look up at Gemma but she's already gone inside. It dawns on me slowly, so slowly that I feel stupid, afterward. This isn't exactly like what happened with Janis, since Gemma and I had never defined things, but damnit, it sure feels like it, my throat feeling tight and my chest aching.

Not only has she chosen Axel, but that sonofabitch has gotten her *pregnant*.

Jackson comes out of the back doors.

"What's going on? Is she drunk?" Jackson asks me, and I put Gemma's phone in his hand.

"No," is all I say, and stalk back into the club to look for the guitarist.

I'm going to kill him.

* * *

Luckily for my arrest record, I don't find Axel in the venue. The tour bus is gone and Jackson and I are stuck but he tells me to go on ahead, that he's meeting someone.

I don't ask any questions. I don't speak a word, actually, because I'm not sure what might come out of my mouth if I open it.

I walk the mile to the hotel, trying to calm down, but it doesn't seem to be working. All I can think about is wrapping my hands around my former friend's throat. Gemma's been so sick and stressed, all because of him. What did he *mean*, talk about the baby? He'd done this, so he has to deal with it, now, and I'm beyond furious.

It's easier to focus on the anger than the ache in my chest, the way there's a voice in the back of my mind saying that if I had only told her earlier, if I'd only made a different choice...

What it boils down to is me not being good enough. I know that Gemma deserves better than an aging rock star with only a two-bedroom house and a shitty 1997 Plymouth to his name. I know she deserves better than the baggage I'll bring with me, worrying about what she's doing every time she's not at home because of how Janis hurt me. Gemma deserves better, but Axel fucking Jermaine isn't better.

It doesn't matter, now. It's over and all I have to do is kill Axel. Well, not kill. I can only maim him because, at the end of the day, I want Gemma to be safe and happy.

That's all I want for the people I love.

There's no point in denying it now, even to myself. I'm in love with Gemma Arden, despite the fact that she's eleven years my junior and my best friend's baby sister. I don't know when it happened, if it was gradual or sudden, but right now it feels like I've been hit by a truck. I love her pale green eyes and all her curves and the way she loves the same snacks as I do. I love the way she sasses me and the way she arches her back beneath me, but it's so much more than that. So much more that I can't even think of her without my heart leaping into my throat.

I'm in love with her and she's pregnant with another man's baby, a man who used to be my friend, and it hurts somewhere deep in my bones, so instead of thinking about it, I focus on my goal.

Find Axel and knock some sense into him. He's going to do right by Gemma if it kills us both.

I finally find him on the fourth floor, walking Gemma to her room, and I tell myself to wait, pause until she closes the door, but when he steps inside with her, I can't help it, I lose it.

I grab the back of Axel's shirt, tugging him backwards.

He lets go of Gemma's arm and stumbles backward, surprised.

"Oh shit, Locke, listen to me, it's not what it looks like-" he starts, and I tackle him to the ground.

"So you didn't knock up my girl?" I bark, and Axel elbows me in the throat and I lose my breath only for a moment before grabbing him again as he tries to crawl away.

We go rolling through the hallway with Axel fighting me the whole way, but I'm taller and I outweigh him by about twenty pounds, so I'm able to pin him. Blood is rushing in my ears and I can barely hear Gemma's yells for me to stop or Axel's protests. Axel is finally able to break through to me by screaming my name, but it barely registers and as he wiggles and almost breaks free, I headbutt him. It hurts my head but it cuts a line across Axel's eyebrow and the blood makes something dark and primal in me satisfied.

Axel groans and I feel ten familiar manicured nails on my shoulder, trying to pull me off. Exhaustion washes over me in a wave, from the sleep deprivation or the heartbreak, I don't know, but I let Gemma pull me off of my ex-friend and sit down on the hotel hallway floor.

"What the fuck is wrong with you?" Gemma yells, and I just look up at her, my head spinning from adrenaline. I regret not accepting the four or five tequila shots I'd been offered back at the venue, because I wish to God I was numb instead of all the anger and pain that's swirling inside me.

"Locke," Axel rasps, sitting up, and of course, Gemma goes to him, pressing a tissue she'd had in her purse against the wound above his eye.

"Don't fucking talk to me," I growl, standing up to loom over him, but Axel's next words shake me more than I'm already shaken and I brace myself against the wall.

"The baby is yours, you fucking idiot," Axel says tiredly, and when I look at Gemma, her pale green eyes widen and I know he's telling the truth.

I put Gemma's phone in her hand, still looking into her eyes. I pause for a moment, wanting to say something, anything.

Instead, I turn and walk away, making it to the elevator as Gemma calls out my name, and brushing past Samuel, who must have heard all the commotion.

There's a mantra going through my head now, over and over. It has for a while, but it's louder than ever, screaming in the front of my head.

Not good enough. Not good enough. Not good enough.

Chapter 24

Gemma

I n the commotion, I get blood all over my white tank
top, so when Samuel sees me, his eyes widen.

I shake my head to let him know I'm not hurt.

"I'm okay, just help me get Axel on his feet."

"What the hell happened?" Samuel asks, and I sigh
heavily.

"I'll explain everything, just get Axel to his room and I'll
come to yours, okay?"

Samuel's brow furrows, but he grabs Axel's hand and
heaves him to his feet.

"I'm okay, it's just right above my eye," Axel complains,
blinking rapidly. Sure enough, there's blood in one of his
bright blue eyes, and I feel awful about it.

I'm still reeling from what happened, the way Locke
had said he had something important to tell me, that he
didn't feel the same way anymore, and I figured he had been
gearing up to break up with me.

I got sick before he could, though, and I didn't realize
that I'd lost my phone until Axel and I made it back to the
hotel. I guess Locke must have seen Alex's text and gotten

the wrong idea. Looking back, it makes sense, him asking me on the bus if I'm seeing anyone else.

I already know that he thinks I'm seeing Axel and to be honest, I've played it up here and there just because it's easier to keep him away from me. It's hard enough seeing him every day, but if I have no buffer, I'm sure I'd have caved by now or told him something I might regret.

I had no idea that it actually affected him this way, though, and I don't know how to feel about what just happened. It's like something out of an action movie, really, the way he tackled Axel and it's all a stupid misunderstanding, anyway.

What did it mean that he called me "his girl" but when he found out the baby is his, he bolted? That doesn't bode well. It's not like I thought we'd live happily ever after, but I thought he might, at least, want to talk about it.

"If you guys hadn't abandoned me after the concert, maybe I could have kept Locke from trying to kill you," Samuel says dryly.

Axel gives me a wry smile as Samuel walks him to his room, and I sigh and follow them, for once not feeling nauseous, even though my face feels hot from all the adrenaline.

I can't stop thinking about how Locke looked at me when I pulled him off Axel. He looked so...hurt, as if I punched him in the throat instead of keeping him from killing our mutual friend.

I feel guilt flow through me. No matter how badly Locke reacted, it's my fault that he thinks that Axel and I are seeing each other. I've been letting him believe that because it served my purposes, and that's a shitty thing to do to someone, even if they don't have real feelings for you.

Hell, no wonder Locke planned to break up with me after the show. No wonder he stormed off the way he did.

I'm the asshole, I think to myself, in wonder, but there's so much more to worry about that I can't even process that thought. I have no idea how Locke feels about kids, no idea how he really feels about me, and no idea what to do next.

Axel must be okay, because he babbles everything that happened to Samuel in an excited tone, and I swear, he must be one of those people who lives for adrenaline. I feel like I've been on one giant ride for about a week now, but Axel seems to be happy to have something to focus on that isn't his ex-wife.

I'm quiet when I walk with Samuel back to his room, and he opens the door for me.

"So, you let Locke Kincaid knock you up, huh?"

"I hate that term," I mutter. "And I just skipped a couple of days on my birth control, I didn't know–"

"You didn't know unprotected sex equals babies?" Samuel drawls, and I huff out a long breath.

"Stop acting like my big brother and give me some real advice," I snap, and then rub my hand over my face.

"I'm sorry. Congratulations." Samuel gives me a sheepish smile. "You're still the baby, after all."

I put a hand on my stomach. "Not anymore," I say softly.

Samuel leads me to the bed, sitting me down on the foot of the bed and turning on the television. I still feel like I'm in a haze, and it helps that he puts on some dumb reality show that I don't have to really focus on.

"You have to tell Jackson."

I look over at Samuel, shocked at his words.

"What?"

"Everyone knows but him, Gemma, you can't just let him find out on his own."

"Fuck, You're right, but...how do I tell him when I haven't even talked to Locke?"

Samuel shrugs. "I can't tell you how to do it, Gem, but he's got to know, and sooner rather than later."

I scoot back on the bed and keep watching some Real Housewives show, not wanting to think about admitting to my brother that I've been not only sleeping with his best friend, but am now pregnant.

"Tomorrow," I state, yawning widely, and Samuel sighs and agrees, sitting down on the couch and throwing me a blanket.

As soon as I wrap it around me, I start to doze off.

* * *

I'm woken up by my phone ringing and I stare at my phone for a long moment before answering my brother's call.

Samuel's passed out on the couch, snoring softly.

"Hey," I greet as cheerily as I can muster.

"Where are you? I've been knocking on your hotel room door for twenty minutes-"

I sigh heavily. "I'm in Samuel's room."

"No one is downstairs for breakfast and I've been waiting for an hour and...wait. You're in...you're where, now?"

I roll my eyes at Jackson's tone and think of reminding him that our father is dead and he doesn't have to fill his shoes, but I decide not to be cruel.

For once, it wasn't Jackson who ruined my social life (and possibly my life in general), but his best friend.

"Samuel's room," I repeat. "I'll be down for breakfast in ten minutes." I pause. "We need to talk."

"About what? About Samuel?" Jackson sounds a little panicked and it almost makes me laugh.

I know he's been worried about Axel, so I guess it's a wild card that I ended up in Samuel's hotel room. Jackson must also know there isn't much chemistry between Samuel and I, though, because otherwise he'd be yelling and banging down the door.

"No. I'll be down soon."

Chapter 25

Locke

I don't sleep, up all night with my mind racing. I'm not good enough for Gemma as it is, how am I going to be good enough to be a father? Even when I'd quit my passion, stopped doing music, and began to work a steady job I wasn't good enough for Janis. What changed since then? The fact that I get a bigger payday when we do a concert? That we sell a few more records and t-shirts? I can't provide for a family on what we make. The only reason I'm keeping my house is because I'd bought it with cash I saved for a wedding that never happened.

Last night, I hurt a good friend because I believed he was doing wrong by Gemma, but how am I going to do right by her? Does she even want me to? I'm certainly not first on her list of priorities, it seems.

I have no idea what I'm going to do about Gemma and the baby, but I do know that I need to apologize to my friend. Unfortunately, Axel won't answer my calls and we end up playing the show in Fairfax without him.

Samuel does a great job on lead guitar, so great, in fact, that he's surrounded by fans who want autographs and he's grinning ear to ear. Samuel might be less extroverted than Axel and Jackson, but he's happy with the attention, especially from the women.

Gemma shows up a little late and Jackson furrows his brow and seems concerned, going to talk to her right after the show. I take my time loading up the equipment on the tour bus since all eyes are on Samuel and I have no idea what to say to Gemma. She catches me outside in the parking garage, clearing her throat to get my attention.

I close my eyes against the way they're burning from exhaustion and emotion, but finally work the bigger amp into the back before turning around to face her.

"So, are we going to talk about this?" She crosses her arms over her chest, which is less intimidating than she wants it to be since she's wearing a Pussycat Dolls t-shirt.

"Didn't seem like you had any plans to talk to *me* about it," I shoot back. I don't realize I'm angry until I am, suddenly.

"I only found out a couple of weeks ago." Her voice sounds softer and less harsh, and I want to be less angry but I'm not.

"*Weeks?* And you told *Axel*? Are you even sure the baby is mine?"

The hurt look on her face makes me regret my words, but it's too late now, in for a penny in for a pound.

"Fuck you for even asking me that."

"What am I supposed to think? You run around with him and avoid me for two weeks and then he's the one who gets to comfort you, gets to talk to you about *my* baby-"

"So, is it yours or is it his? Make up your mind." Her voice has gone cold again and I know I've fucked up but my heart still aches thinking about her with Axel, with or without this baby being mine.

"You say it's mine, it's mine," I say, and I feel a surge of possessiveness, looking down at her hand on her belly. *Damn right it's mine,* I think. *And I want you to be mine, too.*

"It's yours. So, what do you want to do about it?"

I open my mouth to tell her what I'm thinking, that I want her to be mine, but the words stick in my throat. I have issues expressing myself through words, I have my whole life, and so instead, I step forward and wrap my arms around her waist, pulling her close to me just like I had before.

Gemma sighs and it sounds half exasperated but half relieved, somehow, so I twist her in the small parking garage, press her against the tour bus. I'm more careful of her stomach, even though it's no different than it had been a couple of weeks ago when I'd kissed down her body.

"What if you were both mine?" There it is. I say it without thinking and Gemma's brow furrows only for a moment until she wraps her arms around my neck and kisses me, hard, nipping at my lower lip. I think for a moment that pregnancy hasn't changed her sex drive and then she jumps up, clenching her thighs around my waist and I pant against her throat.

There's always a deep, dark part of me that wants to claim the women I sleep with, but it's always been stronger with Gemma, and *now?* It's tenfold. I want to mark her everywhere, make her mine, but I keep my bites soft around the base of her throat and through her shirt where her breasts separate. The last thing we need is for Jackson to find out what's going on, especially since I can barely wrap my head around my feelings for her and this baby.

"Locke," she breathes, and of all the songs I've loved,

this is my favorite, the way she sings out my name when she wants me.

I feel blessed that Gemma has world class legs and knows it, always wearing skirts to our concerts. She's already bunching her black shirt up around her hips and rocking against me, moaning so loudly that it reverberates in the parking garage. I clamp my hand over her mouth and her eyes widen. I remember doing this before, the way I thought she might bite me but she doesn't this time as she didn't before.

Gemma is slippery wet when I slide my fingers through her lower lips and she rocks against me, her cries muffled beneath my palm.

"You gotta be quiet, little bit. Can you do that for me?"

Gemma nods eagerly, her pale green eyes bright in the dim lights of the garage, and I slowly remove my hand and she takes a deep breath in and out.

"Only if you promise not to go easy on me just because I'm pregnant," she says brattily, and I let out a low chuckle.

I work her clit between my thumb and forefinger and she gasps but doesn't make a loud noise, just like I told her. For a brat, she takes orders well, at least in the bedroom. Or, in this case, the parking garage.

The angle is off and I move away to unbutton my pants and Gemma whines softly. I'm still holding her against the back of the tour bus with my body but she slides down, which works because her legs are still wrapped around me and that's just the angle I need to slide inside her.

In retrospect, we should have been using condoms all this time, but the way we had to hook up was so secretive and spontaneous that neither of us thought of it. Now she's pregnant, and it's mine.

Mine, mine, mine, that primal part of me repeats, and

Callie Stevens

my cock is so hard I feel like I might bust inside her embarrassingly fast.

"You're so tight, clenching around me like a vice," I growl, and Gemma's nails rake down my back. If she wasn't so diligent about her manicures, I'd be cut to ribbons by now.

I love dirty talk, but something about how Gemma doesn't talk much, how she just takes what I say and lets her body react, makes my mouth run away with me.

"I'm so close," she whimpers, and I haven't even begun to move yet. She's so hot and wet and responsive, her nipples hard and peaked through her thin t-shirt. Her eyes close and something tightens in my throat.

"Tell me you want me." I order, and her green eyes pop open.

"I...I want you," she gasps, rolling her hips, impatient, but I've got her pinned against the door.

"Tell me you want *only* me," I command, and she frowns at me but she's still rocking her hips. I don't move, clamp my hands down on her hips so that she can't get any friction and she huffs out a breath.

"I only want you," she breathes. "I only want you, Locke, please."

It's the way she says my name that does it, makes my body take over, instead of my brain, and I fuck her at a brutal pace. Her ass slides up and down the back of the tour bus doors.

"You're mine, Gemma, all full with my baby and all mine, yeah?"

"Yes, yes," she pants, her face contorts and I feel her inner muscles clamp down tight around me but I keep my fingers working her clit and she cries out into my mouth when I kiss her deeply.

156

I'm so close to bursting I can feel my heartbeat in my ears, but I keep fucking her through her orgasm and mine, biting a mark onto the side of her neck without thinking about it. As soon as my teeth touch her flesh Gemma cries out and clamps down on me even harder.

"I'm coming again," she whines, and it almost hurts how she pulsates around my spent cock but it's so worth it, the way she goes limp and glassy-eyed. I love the way she looks like this, all fucked out, all *mine*.

I slowly lower her to the ground and she rests her forehead against my chest for a long moment. I rub her back and kiss the top of her head and this is probably the softest moment we've had together after sex. Gemma doesn't like to cuddle, after, at least not with me, which is why I was so surprised when she let me hold her the other day.

I open my mouth to tell her all the things I'm thinking, how I want things to change, how I want to be able to open myself up to love her, but then I hear a familiar voice.

Jackson calls out to Gemma, something about the cover charge cash box, and Gemma flushes and turns away from me, adjusting her skirt as she strides back toward the venue.

It seems like we're always walking away from each other, and I hate it, especially now. It makes me feel like I'm missing a limb or something, some kind of phantom pain from something I never truly had, so I head to the bar.

Gemma's busy and Jackson is as distracted as ever, so I end up drinking a lot more than I plan. I usually feel energized after a session with Gemma, but everything's so different now and all I can think about is how Janis told me we could never have a family and my music career. All I can think about is how I'm not good enough.

A woman, around thirty by her looks and dressed in a

hot pink bodysuit with rhinestones on the neckline, buys me my fifth shot.

"Drummer, right?" Usually, I'd be all over the way she's appreciatively staring at my forearms, but my head is a mess and now spinning with alcohol.

"Do you have kids?" I blurt out, and she blinks.

"Uh, yeah, I do. One," she responds, and I swivel on my bar stool to face her.

"I'm Locke. I'm going to be a dad."

I'm the type of drunk where I don't know exactly what to say until I say it, but the brunette in the pink bodysuit doesn't mind.

"Congratulations..." she trails off, asking for my name, and when I give it to her, she smiles. "Locke. My name is Daniela. My son is four next month."

She puts her small hand in mine to shake, and I appreciate her grace even though it seems she originally approached me to hit on me.

Daniela can tell that I'm in no shape to get home after we chat for a while, so she takes me to her place instead and I pass out on the couch after we talk for hours about Gemma and the baby and what I should do.

* * *

When I wake up, a pair of green eyes are staring at me and the little boy pops his thumb in his mouth when I sit up, his eyes widening at my size.

"It's okay," I say softly, and I notice he's dragging a stuffed lion behind him and wearing lion pajamas. "You like lions, huh?"

He nods eagerly, his eyes lighting up, and for half an hour he babbles to me about lions and prides and how The

Lion King is his favorite movie. It turns out he likes lions because of how they growl and look cool but they also value family. He's precocious for his age and when he makes his way back to his room, I miss him a little, my heart feeling wide and open.

I wonder if that's what our kid will be like, open and loving and chatty. I leave my number on the side table because it's early and I don't want to wake up Daniela. She seemed like a party girl at first, one of those groupies that we deal with on a weekly basis, but she's nothing like some of the women I've met.

She's a good mother, and I know that Gemma will be, too.

I get back to the hotel with a different mindset. I know what I want out of this, and I can only hope that Gemma wants it too.

Chapter 26

Gemma

Locke fucks me up against the back of the tour bus, tells me I'm all his, and then promptly goes to the bar and picks up a thirty-something brunette. Axel and Samuel are both on my ass to tell Jackson what's going on, but at this point I might be arrested for murder before I get a chance to talk to my brother on my own. The talk at breakfast never happened, so he is still in the dark about everything.

I wish I was in the dark about Locke too. I can't even deny to myself that I'm jealous. I'm not just jealous, I'm *furious*. I want to throw a bar stool when I see Locke and the brunette leaving together. He's clearly drunk, leaning into her, and all I can think about is how he seduced that blond bartender the night that everything changed for me.

"What if you were both mine?"

Why would he ask me that and then go do a stupid rockstar thing that makes me question everything I think I know about him? I cannot understand men no matter how I try.

I barely sleep, tossing and turning and having dreams

of Locke fucking both the blond bartender and the brunette from the bar, and when I wake up I'm livid all over again.

I know that I have to tell my brother at some point, but after the tour seems like a better idea. I'm hormonal and traveling and I've already called to make an appointment in three weeks when we'll be back at home. There's only three more shows, the last being Nashville in ten days. We'll be turning in the tour bus to the rental company and flying back home, so I'll have plenty of time to think about it. After all, I have to tell my very protective older brother that I've been impregnated by his best friend, who is eleven years my senior.

Yeah. That's gonna go over well.

I consider ordering breakfast instead of going downstairs for the continental breakfast. I've been hormonal and snippy with everyone, not just Locke, and I feel like kind of an asshole about it. Axel and Samuel have been nothing but helpful ever since I started hooking up with Locke, so I feel particularly bad snapping at one of them.

The problem is, this baby is extremely picky when it comes to food, and something that I love (like onions and peppers with eggs, for example) can suddenly make me want to upchuck all over the place. I'm still feeling nauseous and dizzy off and on, so I want to make decisions that are less likely to make me throw up. I know that everything bagels with the salmon spread they usually have at the Marriott doesn't make me sick, even though I've always hated salmon, so I throw on a pair of sweats and a camisole and get on the elevator.

The good news is that surely Locke will still be at brunette's place; it's early, barely seven in the morning.

I cannot believe my bad luck when he's the only

member of the Spades down at the breakfast bar, making his own waffles with bacon on top.

The waffle maker is, of course, right next to the salmon spread, so I have no choice but to walk up next to him. The smell of cooking pork threatens to make me sick, so I get it as quickly as I can and sit down at a free table.

Locke's been avoiding me like the plague since he found out I'm pregnant, so I'm more than surprised when he sits across from me.

"We need to talk about the baby," he says firmly, and I raise an eyebrow.

"Thought you'd be busy most of the morning," I say nonchalantly, as if it doesn't matter to me one way or the other.

"That's not..." Locke sighs. "Not what we need to talk about."

"You don't have to do anything, you know."

I take a bite of my everything bagel and for once, I don't feel like instantly spitting it out, so I continue. I've been getting decaf coffee, which is a real drag, but I read online that caffeine is bad for the baby. I've been reading a lot online actually, and there's a lot of terrifying things on the internet that I've been babbling to Axel about. He goes really pale any time I mention infant mortality, though, so eventually I started babbling to Samuel instead. These are all things I should be talking to the father of the baby about, but for a couple of weeks I wasn't sure I wanted him to know. And when he learned about it, he ignored me until just now. I look up and Locke is staring at me, his face blank.

"What do you mean, I don't have to do anything?" His voice is low, like he's almost whispering. I want to roll my eyes. I know that we've both been each other's dirty little secret for a while now, but now it irritates me.

"If you don't want to be a part of this, you don't have to be."

"How exactly does that work?" His tone is still low and serious, and I guess he must really be considering this possibility.

That doesn't break my heart at all, nope. Not even a little.

I shrug. "After the tour is over, I'll tell my brother I'm pregnant. I won't tell Jackson that the baby is yours, say it's some guy I picked up while we were on tour. You get to walk away with your hands clean."

"Is this...is this about Axel?"

I look him straight in the eyes because this part, at least, is the entire truth.

"This has nothing to do with Axel. This is about you and me and this baby."

Locke nods slowly and for a moment he doesn't speak and I think the conversation is over.

"Is this what you want?" Locke's searching my face and I know what he wants. I know he just wants to be done with this. He never planned for things to go this far. Hell, neither did I.

I swallow hard, the words sticking in my throat and feeling like acid.

"Yeah. Yeah, this is what I want. You don't like me; I don't like you. We couldn't possibly get along just for the sake of a baby."

"That's how it is," Locke says mysteriously, and he looks dead serious still, that muscle in his jaw twitching. He runs a hand through his hair, nostrils flaring, and that's the only sign that he's feeling any emotion other than...*nothing*.

"That's how it is," I repeat hollowly, fighting tears that threaten at the backs of my eyes.

"That's what you want," he says, repeating my words, and I want to change them. I want to take it all back and tell him that I'm terrified, that I need his help, that I *want*...

But I can't tell him what I want. Not after last night, after he fucked me in a parking garage and then went home with someone else just because he's panicking about my pregnancy.

"That's what I want." My voice sounds shaky.

Locke stares at me a moment longer, searching my face with those big brown eyes, and then he slides the chair back from the table with a screech and storms toward the elevators.

I take in a deep breath through my nostrils to keep from bursting into tears.

That's how it is.

* * *

Despite the way my heart aches, my lack of nausea makes me feel like Wonder Woman and I'm able to pack all my things without the help of Axel or Samuel. Axel and I have been texting and calling, but I haven't actually seen him since his fight with Locke. It's obvious that he's avoiding the drummer, and I certainly can't blame him. Jackson is late, as usual, and Locke is nowhere to be found, so Samuel and I are loading up the tour bus while we wait for the rest of the Spades.

I begin to feel dizzy as I roll my luggage to the tour bus, and Samuel scolds me for putting it in the back myself without waiting for him to help. I grumble but let him put the luggage in. I guess maybe the lack of sleep last night and overdoing it this morning by packing has my vertigo coming back. This baby really wants to put me through the wringer with all the food aversions and cravings and sickness.

I put my hand on my belly. It's way too early to feel any movement, but I feel protective, nonetheless, and I'm considering what Locke said to me and feeling worse and worse as I sit down on the bench in the parking lot.

Samuel finishes loading up and turns around to look at me. His eyes go wide and frightened.

"Gemma?"

I look down at my white shorts and they're stained with red. Suddenly, all the horrible things I'd read start running through my mind and I feel dizzier than ever, my stomach churning. Right now, I'm not thinking of Locke or how hurt I am, all I'm thinking about is my baby and I'm afraid. I'm afraid and there's only one person I trust to be with me when I'm sick and afraid.

"Samuel," I whisper. "I want my brother. Please call Jackson."

My vision starts to black out around the edges and the last thing I remember is Samuel sprinting to keep me from falling on to the pavement.

Chapter 27

Locke

So that's it. It's over and I'll just have Gemma raising a little toddler with my eyes or my smile and have no say in any of it. I'm angry; angrier than I should be, maybe, given that I haven't told her how I feel or what I want.

That's the thing, though. Does it matter? What's most important is for Gemma and the baby to be happy and healthy, and I don't know that I can provide that. We barely know each other, and no matter how much I *feel,* it doesn't matter. Feelings don't pay for diapers and formula. My passion for music won't pay our kid's tuition. My emotions won't make Gemma love me back.

I make plans for the future when I'm feeling unsure, because it's the only thing that keeps me on the ground. Otherwise, I'll lie in bed with a bottle of tequila and the world will stop turning, and that's not how it should work. Not now.

I'm going to quit the Spades. I know that I should finish the tour, keep my responsibilities because I'm the only drummer, but I don't know if I can stand it. I don't know if I can stand seeing Gemma every day, thinking of what I've begun to look at as my future and know I can never have it.

I can't go to my best friend first, as much as I'd like to, because it's up to Gemma when she wants to tell him. I might be furious that she didn't tell me what was going on or that she'd chosen someone else, if that was the case, but I shouldn't have hit him. Axel was my friend before I fell in love with Gemma, and I can't leave the band without making amends, even if I can't bear to be his friend afterward. That's another thing. I'm not just losing Gemma and our child, but the family that I've found. I consider Samuel, Jackson, and even Axel my brothers, in a way, since I never had that sense of family growing up.

I'll call my old boss down at the construction crew and see if he's got a position open, send money to Gemma and the baby every month. She says I can walk away with my hands clean, but that's not true. If I walk away, I lose everything.

I'm hungover and slept only a few thin, alcohol-soaked hours at Daniela's the night before, so I wait until well after nine in the morning to go to Axel's door.

He answers. He's got a band-aid on his forehead and he flinches when he sees me, clearly expecting someone else. Probably Gemma, but I can't think about that too much or I'll hit him again.

He's got his things packed, and I feel lucky that I haven't unpacked my things during all the commotion, since I've already reserved a car to rent to go to the airport.

"I'm not going to hurt you," I tell him, brushing past him into his room, and Axel shuts the door and turns to me slowly, as if I'm a cornered animal.

"Likely story," he says dryly, but he's smiling just a little.

"I came to apologize."

Axel blinks. "What? Locke Kincaid, apologizing? Are you still drunk from last night?"

I shake my head and then pause. "Well, maybe a little, but that's not why I'm here. I need to talk to you about-"

Axel holds up a hand to cut me off, his phone buzzing. "Samuel's calling to bitch at me for not being downstairs already, hold on."

He greets with a "yo!" and I sigh, sitting down on the edge of his unmade bed. I stand up again quickly when I realize that Gemma might have spent the night on that bed, for all I know. That's something that I *definitely* shouldn't be thinking about, if I want to preserve my dignity while leaving the Spades.

"Oh fuck, he knows?" I watch the color drain from Axel's face but I'm not worried. Jackson's definitely going to lose his mind, but I've accepted that, at this point. The next thing he says makes my blood go ice cold, my shoulders stiffen. "The hospital?"

"Is it Gemma?" I ask, loudly, and Axel just stares at me until I take his shoulders in my hands and shake him gently. He nods, and I curse under my breath, pacing around Axel's hotel room.

She doesn't want you. She didn't even call you, I tell myself, but it doesn't matter. I don't care. All I care about is Gemma and our baby being safe. She might not want to see me, but I *have* to know that she's okay.

Axel hangs up the phone and grabs his wallet, shoving it into his basketball shorts and rifling through a duffel bag for a shirt.

I know that I should hurry, go straight to the elevator, but my head feels fuzzy from lack of sleep and everything that's happened in the last few days, and I feel numb and slow. I wonder if I'm in shock or if I *am* still a little drunk.

While Axel lets out a string of curses trying to find a shirt, there's a bang on the door like the police are here and Axel throws it open.

Jackson stands there in sweats and a sleeveless shirt, gaping at Axel, more than likely shocked by the state of his face.

Axel ruins everything by going outside with his hands raised as if in surrender.

"It's not mine!" he blurts out. "I swear to God, I never touched her! Well, not like *that,* anyway."

"What the fuck do you mean, it isn't yours?" Jackson approaches Axel menacingly and backs up. "Are you calling my sister a slut?"

"No! I'm just saying it's not *mine!*"

"Then who the hell-"

That's my cue to leave, bolt for the elevator and hope Jackson doesn't catch me. Yet, I just keep standing there like an idiot as Jackson's gaze follows Axel's and I can see the realization dawn on his face.

"You mother*fucker!*" Jackson yells, and again, I can run. I can run and try to make it, but instead, I just stand there and stare at him.

He hits me right in my nose and it begins to spurt blood immediately. My eyes water, and I make a choking noise in the back of my throat. The pain wakes me up considerably, makes everything seem crystal clear, and I see Axel holding Jackson back by his arms as Jackson struggles and that's when I say it.

"I'm in love with her." It sounds nasally and thick but Jackson stops struggling and Axel slowly lets him go.

Then Jackson tackles me around the waist, and for a guy smaller than me, he sure is sturdy, because I go over like

169

a sack of potatoes, whacking the back of my head on the hallway floor.

"Stop it!" Axel does his level best to keep Jackson away from me, but Jackson just growls and hits him from behind. "Gemma's sick, we need to-" Jackson elbows him in the throat and Axel chokes, stepping away.

I don't even wrestle with Jackson, just repeat myself as if I'm coming to terms with it myself as he punches me in the ribs.

"Aw, jeez, you guys, we're all gonna get arrested," Axel complains, and sure enough, people are coming out of their rooms, watching the fight, some of them on their cell phones.

"I'm in love with Gemma," I say, almost in awe, and then it's lights out when Jackson hits me right on the cheekbone.

* * *

I come to being put into a squad car with Axel and he sighs heavily and rests the back of his head on the seat.

"I didn't even *get* any and I get thrown in jail," he mumbles, I laugh and it sounds tinny to my own ears. I wonder if Jackson gave me a concussion.

If so, I deserve it, that's for sure.

The right way to do things would have been to go to Jackson and tell him that I have feelings for Gemma, to tell him that I wanted to date her and confess that we'd been hooking up. The *right* thing to do would be to talk to Gemma now, but I can't exactly do that from a jail cell or with her in the hospital, and panic rises in my throat just from thinking about it. The cops have taken our phones, so of course, we can't get updates. I can't even think about it too much, it makes me feel like I can't breathe, not knowing what's happening, not knowing if they're okay. I don't know when I started thinking about Gemma as two, when I started thinking of her and the life inside her as mine, but now it's like a part of me is missing.

After two fights and a night of barely sleeping, I'm in and out on the way to the county jail. They separate me from Jackson for obvious reasons, and he's chomping at the bit to get to me even in a jail cell, close to the bars.

"Jack, calm down before they taze you or something," Axel comments tiredly and Jackson gives him a death glare.

"That fucker knocked up my baby sister," Jackson spits out.

"And I made out with her a couple of times, you gonna hang me up by my balls too?" Axel taunts, and I blink, surprised that he's bolder than I am.

I swear, Jackson nearly shakes the bars like Donkey Kong, he's so mad, his face red, his dirty blond hair mussed.

"Are there any of my friends *not* making a play for my sister?"

"I'm pretty sure Samuel isn't," Axel comments idly, and I can't help but laugh.

I've been doing that a lot, lately. I've been laughing and having fun and enjoying my life

instead of just enjoying my music, and Gemma Arden is the one to thank.

"Not a single one of you is good enough for her, and you all kept this from me and now she might be hurt," Jackson growls, and I find myself nodding.

"You're right. I'm not good enough for her," I'm not. And though I know how I feel about Gemma, but I have no idea how she feels about me.

"What you both seem to be forgetting is what *Gemma* wants," Axel comments.

Jackson and I both fall silent at that, and in what feels like half a day but is probably only a couple of hours, an officer comes in to tell us that we've made bail.

"Five grand," Gemma rages the second we pile onto the tour bus. I can't stop staring at her. She looks a bit pale but otherwise okay. "Five grand and now we have to cancel the show, all because you three can't keep from trying to kill each other!"

I whisper to Samuel to find out what happened, and he gives me a sympathetic smile.

"She's okay," Samuel assures me, and when I keep staring at him, my brow furrowed, he adds, "and so is the baby."

I let out a big sigh of relief. I know that I should have asked Gemma about it, but given our last conversation, I don't feel like she's interested.

Even Jackson, as mad as he must be, doesn't argue. He doesn't say anything, actually, heading to the back of the bus and leaving me and Axel in the front with Gemma driving like a maniac.

I keep looking at the profile of her face, her chin with the little dimple in it, and wondering if the baby will have that same dimple, or maybe the one like I have in my cheek. I look away, picking dried blood off my upper lip and avoiding that thought all together.

"Gem," Jackson says to her when she parks in the hotel parking garage, but Gemma shakes her head.

"Not now," she says softly, and Jackson looks down at her and then at me, his face softening just a little, as he gets off the bus. Axel follows with a groan, holding his back, and I do remember hitting him there a couple of times.

Too bad I still can't feel sorry for him. After all, he lied to Jackson, saying that he only made out with Gemma. I know what the score is, and I find a certain dark satisfaction in Axel's sore back.

I walk to the front of the bus and I should just keep going, head into the hotel and be done, text Jackson that I'm leaving so he doesn't try to kill me again, but I can't. I can't seem to move my feet any further than the first step of the tour bus.

"Locke, I'm tired and sick and I need you to get your big ass off the bus-" Gemma snaps from behind me and I turn around to face her and her mouth snaps shut.

I don't realize that I'm crying until she brushes a tear from my cheek. It's strange because since I'm on the first step of the bus, she's nearly my height. It's also strange because I've cried a handful of times in my whole life, and not for two years.

"You're okay?" I ask her, reaching out to touch her belly gently, and she nods slowly.

"Yeah, we're okay. They said that some breakthrough bleeding is normal, especially...especially if you're sexually active." Gemma blushes slightly.

"So, it was my fault?" Fresh tears spring to my eyes and I can't believe I'm not already bolting for the hotel by now. Crying in public is something I've never done before, even those handful of times.

Gemma shakes her head, her beautiful green eyes focused on my face.

"No. No, I'm just supposed to take it easy for a few days."

"I'm so sorry." I move my hands to her hips to bring her closer, pressing my forehead against hers.

I feel like I'm barely there, standing outside of my body, somehow, given everything that's happened. I've been feeling like she's been a million miles away in the hospital, and I realize now that in the back of my head I thought maybe she lost the baby. I'm so grateful that she's here and she and the baby are safe that I don't know how to express it.

"I told you, it wasn't your fault," she murmurs, and I shake my head, pulling away to look at her.

"No. No. I'm sorry for...for everything. I'm sorry that I didn't use protection–"

"So what? You regret this? You regret-"

"No!" I cry out and she shuts her mouth, her bottom lip trembling, her chin jutting out. I want to kiss the little dimple in her chin but instead I just take in a sharp breath through my nostrils and exhale slowly through my mouth like I always do when I'm trying to calm myself. "I don't regret anything. I don't regret *you*, Gemma, and I won't. Not ever. I know that you have other plans. I know that you don't...that you don't want me."

Gemma's eyes are the color of the sea when they're swimming with tears. She's so beautiful and I feel so stupid for not noticing it six months or a year ago.

"Locke," she starts, and I love hearing her say my name, but in this context, it hurts. I don't want her to pity me, that hurts more than her rejection.

"I know that you want me to walk away, little bit, but I *can't*. I don't want to. I want to be a part of this baby's family, just like the guys are a part of mine."

"You...you do?" Gemma's voice sounds hesitant and shaky.

I shake my head and her face falls, so I take her hands, kissing her knuckles.

"Not just that. Not just the baby. I want to be yours and I want you to be mine, Gem."

"What are you saying, Locke?" Gemma's still got her

chin jutted out like she's mad at me but there are tears rolling down her cheeks and she doesn't remove her hands from mine.

"I'm saying..." I pause and take in another deep breath. "I'm saying that I'm in love with you, Gemma."

She catches her bottom lip between her teeth and I thumb it. She huffs out a breath and I can't help but laugh even though my heart is in my throat since she hasn't responded.

She stares at me and it feels like my whole life is in her small hands.

Chapter 28

Gemma

I knock softly on the hotel door, taking in a deep breath, not exactly excited about what's about to come.

My brother answers the door right away and grabs my hand, pulling me inside and forcing me to sit down on the bed.

"Are you okay?" he asks, his brow furrowed, and I smile.

"I'm fine. The baby's fine, too."

"Good," Jackson says and then his face turns sour. "Now, you wanna tell me what in the *fuck* you were thinking, hooking up with my best friend?"

I sigh heavily. " I wasn't thinking, honestly. And if it helps, at first I was trying to hook up with your *other* friend."

"Yes, yes, I know," Jackson groans. "I've heard, and that's no less gross."

I tilt my head, looking at him for a long moment and he sighs.

"You look so much like Mom when you do that."

It's bittersweet, knowing how much I look like our

mother and that she's gone, but I'm glad to have her no-nonsense attitude and grounded personality. Jackson is more like our father. Dreamy, with his head in the clouds, and reactive. I think things through, analyze things, or at least, I used to do that. Now, it seems like I'm flying by the seat of my pants, but it's good to know that I can still analyze my big brother.

"Does it matter who it is?" I ask. "Or would you be angry no matter what?"

"I'm not...I'm not *angry* with you, Gem."

"You're not?" I feel my bottom lip trembling and I hate it. Jackson doesn't exactly try to fill the shoes of our parents but he *has* taken care of me for years.

"I'm angry at *Locke,*" he elaborates, and I frown. Jackson sighs. "I'm not even exactly angry at him anymore, I'm just upset that neither of you came to me about this situation."

"Jack, don't pretend like you wouldn't have hit him if he'd come to you and said that he wanted to hook up with your little sister."

"Of *course* I would have, but it would have been a lot less hard than I hit him after he lied to me for weeks and then got my little sister pregnant."

"It's not like he meant to get me pregnant, Jackson, he-"

"He fell in love with you," Jackson comments flatly, and I blink, looking up at him in shock. "Yeah, he told me."

"Guess I know what it's like to be the last to know," I comment dryly, and Jackson laughs.

"The thing is, Gemma, Locke is a good guy. He really is. Sometimes, he loses his way, but we all do, now and again. It's not like I hate the idea of you with Locke, it's just...it's hard for me to look at you and not remember what you were like at fifteen when..."

Jackson trails off. We don't talk about it, how our parents died, what we went through. We haven't really talked about it since it happened.

I put my hand on his shoulder. "I know. I know, Jack. But I'm not fifteen anymore."

Jackson shakes his head, laughing softly. "You're not. I know that. You're a lot older at twenty-one than I was at twenty-five, but Gem, there's so much life you haven't lived. So many things you haven't done, and that's...that's partially my fault."

I raise an eyebrow. "Partially?"

"Okay, okay, *mostly*," Jackson sighs. "I know I've been too protective, and I know that you had to grow up fast. I took care of you when we were kids but you've taken care of me as an adult a lot of times, and don't think I don't appreciate it, Gem."

I'm tearing up again. Damn hormones. I've never been much of a crier, but now it's like the waterworks turn on at the slightest thing.

"I'm sorry I didn't tell you," I start, and Jackson sits up straight, holds up his hand to stop me.

"I'm not finished. You didn't tell me because I've tried to be Dad instead of being your big brother, and I understand that. But I need to know one thing."

He gives me a hard look, that one that tells me that I better tell the truth or I'll be grounded, and I smile a little, thinking that he's more like Dad than he thinks.

"Is this what you want?" he asks, taking my hand. "Do you want this baby, to be a mother so young?"

I nod, not trusting myself to speak.

Jackson is still giving me that look, though, and I know he's not finished.

"Is *Locke* what you want? Do you feel the same way about him as he does about you?"

I take in a deep breath, close my eyes, and tell my brother the truth.

* * *

It's been almost a year since the first tour started and there's been so much success since then. The Spades blew up on Tiktok and Soundcloud after the tour and Axel has become our in-house social media influencer, posting clips of originals, playing covers and acoustic versions of Spades' songs on his guitar having Samuel with him in some of them as well. He hasn't given up on his ex and other than seeing him every two weeks for garage rehearsal, there hasn't been a lot of time to speak with him one on one since the baby was born. I've been busy, and I guess he has too.

We kept playing our shows, up until my last trimester, and all hell broke loose when I went into labor at a concert, so baby Cain was quite literally born into the life. The guys decided this was a good time for the band to go on a concert hiatus, in order to prepare their first real album.

Having sold out all our merchandise on our first tour, and with all the new fans we have on social media, we expect to get a good deal of money when their official album hits Spotify and iTunes. There are even talks about an international tour, and that is on the horizon, but for now, the comeback tour would be local.

Jackson still kind of hates the idea of me growing up, but he sure loves Cain, even stayed up a few nights helping me feed and diapering. The Spades are a family and the fact that we are all even closer now, despite everything that had gone on during the tour, shows how much we all love each other.

As for me....well...I'm in the same place I was around a year ago (roughly), except now it's my ass against the inside stall door of a club women's bathroom in Las Vegas with a man kissing my throat and neck, groaning against my flesh.

"The last time I did this was with my baby's father," I groan as he rolls his hips against me.

He lifts his head, grinning at me, a dimple popping out in his right cheek.

"Oh yeah, what happened to him?"

"He's around somewhere," I drawl, running my fingers through his hair, which has gotten longer in the past year.

"He's in the band or something, right?"

"Drummer," I comment.

"Boring," my beau says, bunching my skirt around my hips. "Should have gone for a guitarist."

I let out a peal of laughter that ends in a moan when he slides his fingers up inside me. I can never get enough...and since having the baby (after the six-weeks mark, of course) every time is almost like losing my virginity again, even though that night is still in bits and pieces given all the alcohol I ingested that night.

"I *tried*," I insist, and he frowns, pulling away and stilling his fingers inside me.

"Do you regret that you chose me, little bit?"

I roll my eyes. "You know I don't, Locke. You're the only man for me, you know that."

"Damn straight," he grunts, and slides inside me.

"God, I love it every time," I groan, clenching around him.

"So damn tight." Locke tugs at my hair so that he can suck marks on to my neck.

After all those weeks keeping things secret, Locke has a penchant now for marking a necklace of hickeys around my throat and collarbone. I say it's tacky but he says he wears the claw marks on his back with pride and all the marks I give him, so I just cover mine up in public with makeup.

Locke doesn't like it, always rubs the makeup off as soon as I get home, but I've learned to deal with it.

"Tell me you want me," Locke commands, and it's a repeat, my favorite re-run.

"I want you," I say easily, and Locke kisses me hard on the mouth, our teeth almost gnashing together, and then presses his forehead against mine.

"Tell me you love me," he says, softer, almost asking this time, and I smile.

"I love you, Locke Kincaid."

These soft moments are usually followed by some mix between primal and romantic sex, but the sound of the outer bathroom door swinging open stops everything.

Locke freezes, and I whine loudly and he clamps his hand over my mouth and suddenly I'm transported back to a year ago when we were sneaking around, keeping our relationship and my pregnancy a secret.

It doesn't do much to stop my hips from rolling against him, after all, the sneaky part was one of the hottest things about Locke, at least in the beginning.

"Ten minutes until show time," Axel says dryly. "I'm covering my eyes, so just put your clothes on and get *out* here, Locke."

Locke groans and I giggle, the sound muffled against his palm. Locke gives me a look that I absolutely live for, one that makes me know that the next time we're alone together, I'll have a great time.

Locke remains slightly salty about Axel, but it's tit for

tat since Locke started up a friendship with *Daniela*, the woman that he went home with the night before he confessed his feelings to me. Granted, her little boy, Leo, is absolutely lovely and Cain will grow up almost viewing him as a big brother, given all their playdates, but every time she calls Locke instead of me (which isn't often), I feel a burst of jealousy. Of course, I think the story of him meeting her son, Leo, is adorable, but I hate the idea that Locke slept with someone else.

Locke thrusts his hips and rocks into me one final time, making me gasp, before he slowly pulls out, adjusting his clothes and pulling my skirt down my thighs with a sigh.

"I can't believe your ex-boyfriend cockblocked me," Locke jokes.

"You tried to do it plenty of that to him last year," I remind him, and Locke grumbles, running a hand through his hair since I'd mussed it.

He opens the stall and I walk out first.

"Axel cockblocked himself, from what he tells me," Locke responds as I wash my face in the sink, and I look in the mirror, seeing him standing behind me, his arms around my waist.

I raise an eyebrow.

"Did he tell you the whole story?"

Locke shrugs. "Most of it, I think. He didn't give me any details so I wouldn't bust open that scar on his eyebrow again."

I laugh a little. "Yeah, Daniela doesn't give me details, either. She did try to tell me that you slept on the couch, though, which kind of pissed me off. You didn't give me any details about *Daniela* either, except that you slept on the couch," I scoff. "I don't know why you lied about it. There's no reason to lie about it, after all this time. We weren't technically together, after all."

Locke slowly removes his hands from my waist, frowning.

"I did sleep on the couch. Little bit, nothing happened with Daniela. We just talked about you and Cain and then I passed out."

My eyes widen in shock and I turn around and hit him softly on the shoulder with the heel of my hand.

"You mean I've been seething about this for *a year* and you didn't even sleep with her?"

Locke scoffs. "You're one to talk. You get to be *best friends* with your ex-lover and you get mad at me if I get snippy about it."

I stare at him for a moment and then erupt into a peal of giggles, holding my stomach.

"What? It's not funny, Gemma, I-" Locke actually looks angry and I can't even listen to what he's saying because I'm laughing so hard.

"I never slept with Axel, you idiot. You took my virginity."

Locke makes the *most* comical face, and I swear I'm going to fall over laughing.

He grabs me around the waist and picks me up, swinging me around before kissing me soundly on my laughing mouth.

"I knew it," he says, and I know that's a damn lie given all the fights we've had about Axel calling me to ask for advice. "You've always been mine."

I let him have it, though, since we're already late for Jack and the Spade's big comeback concert.

Locke makes his way backstage and I stand right in front, elbowing a groupie out of the way to get my spot. It feels good to have everyone back on stage again: Axel, who looks healthier than he has in years, Samuel with his hair cut short and a big grin on his face, my brother, as big and loud as ever, and Locke Kincaid, giving me a sly smile from the back of the stage as the lights go up. Locke hits the snare drum and the sound makes my skin tingle.

As Keyed Up cues in I think of how we were all those months ago. And guess what?

I guess I like him, after all.

Thank you for reading Accidental Baby For My Brother's Best Friend.

If you loved this book, then you'll LOVE Accidental Secret Daddy...
Read on for a preview...

Chapter 29

Accidental Secret Daddy

My Rockstar ex-husband left me a parting gift after our breakup- a bun in the oven.
And he just doesn't know it yet.

He was my one and only...until he chose his rockstar lifestyle over me.

When his tour brought him back to town, and became my next door neighbor, my baby bump is on full display.

Just my luck!

I lied and told him it wasn't his.

He'd never choose us over the Rockstar lifestyle.

But every time I see his piercing blue eyes and tattooed, muscular body, my heart begs me to reach out.

I can't risk the chance of rejection again for me, or our child...

. . .

Continue to read Accidental Secret Daddy...

Chapter 1

Axel

Returning to my hometown after all those weeks away on tour feels surreal. Everything looks the same, but somehow, it feels different. It might be because I've been in all these big cities performing, but I think mostly is because there is one major difference. Harley isn't here.

Harley Telman has been the love of my life since I was sixteen years old and she moved almost next door to me. From the moment I met her, I couldn't see anyone else. Hell, I *still* can't, no matter how many groupies throw themselves at me.

The tribal tattoo in my arm is a constant reminder of all I had and lost. The dates camouflaged into it mark the happiest days of my life. The day she said yes to being my girl and the day I made her mine forever. Or so I thought. Regardless, Harley will always be a part of me. Like she's imprinted in my very soul.

I shake my head, trying to rid myself of thoughts of her. The pain is too raw still. It has been five months since I saw her last and it still hurts as much as if it had been yesterday.

Chapter 1

But I can't dwell on that now because I have an important meeting with a real estate agent.

While I was on tour, things weren't as bad because I had multiple distractions, including endless amounts of booze, the shows, my friends, and the never-ending supply of bed partners. But coming home to the memories of her is crushing me. I can't stay in that house. Our house.

So, I need a new place to stay. Thank God for Theresa, my realtor friend. She told me of this little duplex that should be perfect for me, or so she says. Since I started taking care of social media for the band and recording covers and unplugged versions of our songs, I realized I need a space that will allow me to have a room just for my equipment. The band is doing well, so now is the perfect time to take the risk and buy a new place.

If I weren't doing the social media stuff, a bedroom and a bathroom with a little kitchen would be more than enough, because there is no way I'll ever get to share my life with anyone ever again. In the span of eleven years, I found and lost my soulmate. There is no way I'll ever want anyone other than her.

I don't much look forward to living right next door to someone, but maybe having someone around will help me. After these months of always having the guys and Gemma around, I think I might be lonely living by myself, but it's not like I have much of a choice.

The realtor assures me that the other occupant is a lovely woman, and she hinted that she's around my age. Maybe we can become friends and it'll be fun. At least, that's the hope.

I'm starving by the time I make it to the little duplex that I'm touring on the request of my realtor, and I see her there, smiling and waving, as I pull up on my motorcycle, parking with plenty of room for the U-Haul trailer behind it. I take my helmet off slowly, appreciating the back view of the woman standing in the yard next to Theresa.

Holy shit. She looks good from the back and she's got all this blonde hair in curls down her back, which I have to admit, does something for me. Reminds me of Harley's mane of hair and how much I loved seeing it sprawled on my pillow.

As I approach Theresa, I try to shake myself off thoughts of Harley. My eyes stay on the woman and I realize that she's very pregnant, probably ready to pop. Not sure how friendly we can become if she'll soon have all her time consumed by a mini-human being, but I love people and there is no harm in saying hi, I guess.

At my approach, she turns and smiles at me, as I stop right in front of Theresa and her, holding my helmet in one hand.

When our eyes connect, my helmet drops to the ground.

It has been five long months since the last time I heard her voice. Longer since I looked at her face. And now, here she is, right in front of me, blinking at me with those big blue eyes of hers, and she's *pregnant*.

What the *fuck?*

Continue to read Accidental Secret Daddy...

Chapter 2

Harley

This cannot be happening to me. Axel Jermaine cannot be standing in my yard. And he's staring at my stomach like I have an alien inside me instead of a baby.

"Harley, this is -" Theresa starts, and I hold up my hand to stop her.

"We've met," I say dryly, and Axel barks out a laugh.

"You could say that," he responds, and there's a bite in his voice. He's mad.

I can't really blame him. After all, I have been radio silent for months. I can feel the blood leaving my face, waiting for him to put it together.

"Where is he?" he asks in a clipped tone, although his face doesn't show his distress. Axel's really good at hiding his emotions when the situation calls for it.

I pause, confused, until I finally realize that he thinks I've got some boyfriend or new husband around that got me in this situation, which is both sad and a relief. Sad because he thinks I'd do that. A relief because as long as he thinks that, I don't have to worry about him putting the dates together from the last time we were intimate.

I shrug. "Around."

Theresa stares at me but she doesn't say anything. Bless her.

Theresa Santos and I became close since I moved into the duplex, mostly because I was on my own and terrified, trying to keep my pregnancy a secret from all the people close to me. She knows it's just me and the baby, but she doesn't know my past or who Axel is to me.

All my friends know my history with Axel, and they'd know immediately what was going on, so I isolated myself from them. From everyone, really, preferring to be alone than risking my secret. I'm the only one who can be trusted, because there's no way in hell I ever want my ex-husband to find out he knocked me up.

As much as it pains me and my heart breaks at the thought, Axel and I are done. I had my reasons and those haven't changed. There is no way a baby is going to change things or make them any better.

There's a muscle twitching in Axel's jaw as he keeps staring at me, and something like hurt flashes across his face when he meets my eyes. It's so quick anyone but me would have missed it. I look away, my heart sinking. I'm still too attuned to his moods, as mercurial as they are. And the thought of hurting him hurts me tenfold.

Fuck. I thought I was almost over him. The way my heart is aching tells me I'm wrong.

"Um, is there something I'm missing, here?" Theresa asks.

"Nope," Axel responds. "I'll take it."

My eyes shoot to his, but he won't look at me now.

"What do you mean, you'll take it?" I ask, dread filling me. He can't stay here. Axel shrugs.

"It's a nice place. I like the lawn." He hasn't even seen the inside of the duplex.

Anxiety and anger rise inside me. I know he's just doing this to get a rise out of me, that he wants to stay here to try and figure out who got me pregnant. But that can't happen. There is a reason I had to stay away from him. And now I have my baby to think about too. My child needs to be the most important thing in my life now, and I can't focus on her if I have to see him every day.

"Fine, I'll move out," I shoot back, and Theresa gives me a pained look.

"Harley, I'm all booked up for the summer. There isn't a single two-bedroom available anywhere in town," she says slowly.

Fuck. I need a two bedroom for the nursery. As I contemplate what the hell I'm going to do, Axel shakes Theresa's hand and takes the key.

The next thing I know, Theresa is leaving and he's moving boxes out of the U-Haul into the left side of the duplex as I'm standing there, shell-shocked. I watch his biceps bulge as he picks up a large suitcase, and my mind tries to run away from me, taking me back to a different time. A time when we couldn't stand being apart for a second.

I look away. I have to. There is no way I will allow my hormones to get the best of me. Axel Jermaine shattered my heart. Yeah, he's hot, but that's not enough to make up for how he is.

It's not even like Axel is a bad guy. He's a good guy, but just not the right guy for me. I can't handle all the partying and the girls hanging off his arm. It's not that I don't trust him, though Axel has always been a big flirt. It's that I don't trust

Chapter 2

them. The fans. The women constantly throwing themselves
at him. I hate that I am that insecure, but my past growing up
taught me that men can't always be trusted, no matter how
much you love them or how much they claim to love you.

At first, we were together all the time. From the time I
moved a bit down the street from him, he had been
enchanted by me. Me? Not so much. His flirty ways always
had me doubting if I was enough. From the moment we
met, and for four years, we were glued at the hip. Right after
he joined the band, he proposed to me, and that was one of
the happiest days of my life. Becoming his wife was a dream
come true, but it soon became a nightmare.

"When do I get to meet the lucky guy?" Axel asks,
jolting me out of my head.

"What?" I ask, confused, and Axel scoffs.

"The daddy. He must be proud," he drawls, and I give
him a hard look.

"You won't. He doesn't come around here," I tell him,
and Axel stares at me for a long moment.

He takes in a deep breath, and I swear I can tell he's
inwardly counting to ten. Axel's always had a temper, and
honestly, I'm surprised that he's taking it this well. In fact, it
makes my heart sink. If he's barely even jealous, does he
even care anymore? Maybe he met someone else on that big
tour Jack and the Spades did. And why do I even care,
anyway? Why does it crush me to even consider that?

"Good," he grumbles, and I take in a breath of my own.

"What about you? I don't want girls coming in and out
of here," I shoot back, and Axel grins.

"Not that you can dictate who I can or can't have in my
house, since I'm paying for rent same as you, but don't
worry, sweetheart. They rarely stay the night."

He's right, of course, but that doesn't stop anger from

boiling up in me, something bitter at the back of my throat. I huff out a breath and head inside, tears springing to the backs of my eyes. I've always been an angry crier, and I hate that about myself. It's only gotten worse with all the hormones, and I certainly don't want Axel to think I'm upset instead of just mad.

Before I can escape inside, he asks, "How far along are you?"

"Going on seven months," I lie. I'm eight months. It's been precisely eight months, two days, and seventeen hours since this baby was made. Eight months, two days, seventeen hours since I was with a man, but who is counting. Thing is, he can't know that. Ever.

Axel grunts, looking away from me. "You didn't waste any time."

"Why should I? I doubt you did," I retort, and I can feel Axel's sharp blue eyes driving a hole on my back. But I can't face him.

"You think you know everything, don't you, Harl?" he says mysteriously, and his heavy footsteps retreat, probably heading toward the U-Haul.

I take the opportunity to sneak into the house, breathing hard and trying not to cry. When we got married, I had dreamed of a loving family with Axel. Being with him forever, our children running and playing and wreaking havoc all around us as we happily watched them grow. Gently setting my hand on my belly, I contemplate the fact that my dream was an illusion. I know now I'll never stop loving Axel, and this little one is the only part I'll ever have of him. I wish he could be part of this, of us, but his priorities lie elsewhere. And I may not be able to change that but there is no way my baby will grow up feeling like she isn't the most important person in the world. I rather she thinks

Chapter 2

her dad died or went away than feel like she is an afterthought in his life.

Noise from outside draws my curiosity and it only takes a minute before I get go peeking out of my blinds to see him carrying more boxes inside.

He pauses to tug off his shirt. *Damnit.* I can't seem to look away, watching the muscles in his abdomen and chest as he wipes sweat from his brow with his T-shirt. It reminds me of when he was on stage, after a solo, when he'd grin and throw his sweaty T-shirt right at me. Axel is perfect for lead guitar, perfect for the stage, and for most of my life, I thought he was perfect for me.

I want to call my best friend, Charlotte, but I haven't talked to her in months. She'd even sent me a letter at my parents' house, pleading with me to call her, but I'd kept ignoring her calls, kept telling my mother to tell her that I wasn't feeling well when she finally showed up. I can't call her, as badly as I need my best friend.

Instead, I call Theresa, my only friend now.

"Harley Telman, what the hell is going on with you and Axel?" Theresa answers, and I almost want to laugh.

I'm glad that she's my friend and not just my landlord, that's for sure.

"He's my ex-husband," I say, and Theresa gasps dramatically. She must still be in the car, on the way back to the office, because it's only been an hour since Axel showed up.

"He's your *what?* Is he...is he the father?" she asks.

I bite my lip, thinking, but in the end, I decide that it's best to keep this secret to myself, because no one can slip if no one knows.

"No, he's not. He's just a pain in my ass," I respond, and Theresa lets out a low whistle.

196

Chapter 2

"I noticed there was some tension between you two, but I never imagined you used to be *married*."

"You've got to get him out of here," I say firmly, and Theresa pauses on the line.

"Is he a bad guy? Was it an abusive relationship?"

"No, no," I say instantly. Axel would never lay a hand on me, despite his short temper. That was never the problem. I never doubted his love for me. He was the sweetest, most loving man ever. "Nothing like that. It just didn't work out."

"I can't kick someone out of a duplex they paid for just because you have history with him, Harley. You've got to give me something more," Theresa says with a sigh.

I worry my bottom lip between my teeth. "Then you've got to find me something else, Theresa. I can't live like this, not with him right next door..." Tears start to well in my eyes again and I angrily wipe my eyes. Stupid hormones.

"I'll keep an eye out, but it's going to be a while, Harl. Like I said, everything's booked up for the summer."

I heave a deep sigh. "Thank you for looking."

We chat for another few minutes and then I hang up, rubbing my hands across my face. I look over at the half put together crib in the corner and sigh again. I hate DIYs and I've never been particularly handy.

I can't help myself from peering out the window again, and this time, Axel is on his motorcycle and looking right at me. Part of me wants to snap the blinds closed, but I'm not sure if he can see me from this distance.

There's this pull in my stomach as we meet eyes, some kind of line of fate drawing me back to him, but I push it away. Just like before, something flashes across his face, so quickly anyone else might have missed it. I'm not sure if it's

197

anger or hurt or both, and I almost expect him to get off his bike and come stalking up to the front door.

My breath catches in my throat. Do I *want* him to come to the door? Do I want him to take me in his arms, tell me everything is okay? Yes. No. Maybe...

Finally, he breaks eye contact, putting on his helmet. He takes off, tires squealing as he pulls the motorcycle and the U-Haul into the street.

I finally let out the breath I've been holding and my mind clears. I can't want him. We've been there before and there was only hurt for me at the end. Axel Jermaine, living no more than a hundred feet from me and my baby is a recipe for disaster.

How am I going to get out of this?

Continue to read Accidental Secret Daddy...

Printed in Great Britain
by Amazon

18592886R00120